"I'm so glad

He grinned. "Of course. It's what friends do."

Maybe *friends* was a stretch considering the time gap, but Allie no doubt understood his intent.

They ate in silence for a while. Steve watched her. She ate with considerably more enthusiasm now that her trouble was on the table. It wasn't every day someone was visited by the FBI and accused of the murder of a man they didn't know in a place where they hadn't been in years. She had every right to be upset and defensive. He appreciated that she had enough faith in him to sound reasonably relaxed and open in spite of the concerns likely reeling in her mind.

Steve pushed his plate aside and rested his forearms on the table. She did the same, her gaze on his, searching. The pulse at the base of her throat fluttered again. She was visibly braced for his conclusions.

"I don't practice criminal law," he explained. "I primarily counsel and advise the agency on operational matters. I can represent you if that's what you want."

"Yes!" Her relief was palpable. "Please."

Reader Note

If you've read my Colby Agency stories, you know the series is my longtime favorite. I hope you enjoy this one.

When writing stories set in real places, it's often necessary to change things up a little. Add a house for the hero or heroine on a certain street. Drop a diner like Red's into the middle of town. Of course, it's important to have public services in the story. I often have police officers or other folk who play important roles. All are fictional, just another character living in my head. Most important, none of the characters I create who do bad things are ever based on a real person. I have the deepest respect and greatest admiration for all public and civil servants as well as elected officials. Sometimes it just works best for the story to make one a not-so-nice character...maybe even a villain. Enjoy!

ALIBI FOR MURDER

DEBRA WEBB

Alibi for Murder

Harlequin

INTRIGUE

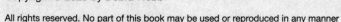

Recycling programs for this product may not exist in your area.

Harlequin® INTRIGUE™

ISBN-13: 978-1-335-69014-2

Alibi for Murder

Copyright © 2025 by Debra Webb

Harlequin Enterprises ULC
22 Adelaide St. West, 41st Floor
Toronto, Ontario M5H 4E3, Canada
www.Harlequin.com

Printed in Lithuania

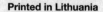

MIX
Paper | Supporting responsible forestry
FSC® C021394

Debra Webb is the award-winning, *USA TODAY* bestselling author of more than one hundred novels, including those in reader-favorite series Faces of Evil, the Colby Agency and Shades of Death. With more than four million books sold in numerous languages and countries, Debra has a love of storytelling that goes back to her childhood on a farm in Alabama. Visit Debra at debrawebb.com.

Visit the Author Profile page at Harlequin.com.

CAST OF CHARACTERS

Allie Foster—Allie has no family. She lives alone, works from home...never goes anywhere. An unexpected knock on her door turns her life upside down. Suddenly she's a murder suspect and everything that's happening, all the secrets and lies, appear to be related to her family's past.

Steve Durham—He grew up in Allie's neighborhood. He's now an advising attorney at the Colby Agency. Despite the fact that he hasn't seen the shy girl who helped him survive pre-calculus in high school in years, he rushes to her rescue...but can he save her from a past she didn't know existed?

Thomas Madison—The murder victim... No matter that he's dead, he may be the only one who can prove what really happened.

Jesus Rivero—Once a hotshot reporter on the verge of national fame, he knows more than he's sharing. But is he the key to Allie's salvation...or the path to her doom?

Special Agents Elon Fraser and Uma Potter—The two FBI agents are the ones who bring the trouble to Allie's door. Can she trust them? Or are they only interested in solving their case?

Lucille and Dennis Reger—The mystery couple in Allie's family photos. They might know the truth...if she can find them.

Victoria Colby-Camp—The head of the Colby Agency. Victoria never backs down from danger. She and her agency are Allie's one true hope of surviving this storm.

Chapter One

Woodstock, Illinois
Friday, June 6
Foster Residence
Ridgeland Avenue, 5:30 p.m.

"I hope you'll complete the survey when you receive it. We at GenCorp are always here for you, twenty-four seven."

Allie Foster ended her final call for the day—for the next ten days, actually—and removed the wireless headset. She exhaled a big breath, stood from her desk and stretched. There was something about Fridays, even when you didn't have plans for the weekend or her first vacation in years happening.

Fridays marked a milestone of completing a week's work, of having two days off ahead. Well, ten in this case. It was a good feeling.

Or it would be if she had plans of any kind. Sadly she did not.

"Woo-hoo," she grumbled as she placed the headset on her desk. She shut off the desk lamp and walked out of her office. She was taking a vacation and going *nowhere*.

How exciting was that?

She would do yard work and maybe finally paint her

bedroom. A really old-fashioned getaway from work. Wasn't she the globetrotter?

Admittedly, Allie had always been a little on the old-fashioned side. Came from being raised by much older parents, she supposed. Technically, they were her grandparents. Her parents had died in a car accident when she was a toddler. She had only the faintest memories of them.

Frankly, she wasn't entirely certain she remembered them at all, she decided as she slowly descended the stairs. The framed photos of her family, her parents when she was little and her grandparents as well as her over the years, lined the wall along the stairs. There was a strong likelihood that the stories she'd heard growing up and these photographs along with the many family albums carefully curated by her grandmother were the actual memories she recalled.

Allie banished the idea and focused on mentally shrugging off the workweek and the stress that often went with providing patient services. Answering calls all day might not sound like a tough job, but these were questions from patients who were, for the most part, terminally ill. Either they or a family member had questions about their medications or their appointments or simply what they should do next. GenCorp was a huge medical operation. The services provided extended across the country and involved cutting edge, sometimes experimental, pharmaceuticals, procedures and end-of-life patient care.

There were always questions and emotions and financial issues. And although, as a nurse, Allie's job was to answer questions regarding the medical side of things, that didn't prevent frustrated patients and family members from spilling conversations over into the other difficult parts of terminal illnesses. Life during those times was complicated and painful.

What she needed now was to relax with her evening glass of wine and chocolate bar.

"Better than sex."

Probably not true, but it had been so long since she'd had sex, she wasn't entirely sure. But to believe this was the case made the idea of no prospects far more palatable and much less depressing.

No one's fault but your own, Al.

Relationships didn't generally come knocking on the door. One had to actually put in some effort to acquire one.

Not going there.

Out of habit, she walked around the first floor and checked the windows and doors. Woodstock's crime rate was fairly typical for a town of its size. Not a big town, more on the small side. Still, decades ago her grandparents had a security system installed. It wasn't the best, but it remained serviceable. Although it was no longer monitored, it made a long, loud noise when breached. Since Allie took over the house five years ago, she hadn't bothered changing it. She wasn't really paranoid about crime or the possibility of intruders. She preferred to consider herself careful.

Or maybe she was paranoid since she hadn't changed the fact that there were three—count them, three—deadbolts on the front door. As a teenager, she'd always wondered why there were three on the front door and none on the back. And she had always intended to add one to the back but never bothered.

Which, all things considered, likely made her every bit as paranoid as she'd been certain her grandparents were.

Satisfied that the house was secure, she wandered into the kitchen. One cupboard was dedicated to her favorite bottles of red. The drawer beneath the counter in that same spot held her chocolate stash. She was a simple girl. Many years from now, hopefully, when she was found dead and no doubt alone in the house, no one would think less of her for having plenty of wine and chocolate on hand.

Maybe she was also slightly paranoid about running out of either.

Laughing at herself, she removed the cork from the bottle. Any burglar would no doubt be disappointed if he broke into her home. Wine and chocolate—well, and her computer—were the only valuables in the house. There was no stash of cash or collection of coins. No jewelry, unless you counted the costume stuff her grandmother had adored. No weapons except the BB rifle her grandfather had used for scaring off pesky squirrels and birds from his garden out back. Not that he ever hit one or even tried. It was all about the noise of hitting something nearby, he had explained. It worked every time, he'd insisted.

Allie retreated to the living room with her glass of wine and the chocolate bar. The old box-style television still stood in the corner of the room. It was the perfect size for her aquarium. As she passed, she checked the auto feeder to ensure it held an adequate amount.

"Hello, Nemo and friends." She tapped the glass and smiled as they darted around.

She frowned at the collection of dust on the dinosaur of a television. This was something else she needed to do on her vacation. Dust, not replace the set. She hadn't watched it in years, even before it died. The news was far too depressing, and the entertainment industry had stopped making decent movies ages ago.

She picked up her book from the side table and opened it to the next chapter. Books never let her down.

Who needed television when they had books?

The buzz of the doorbell made her jump. For a moment, she felt confident she must have imagined it. She had no deliveries scheduled. No one ever came to her door, not even the neighbors' children selling cookies or doing other fundraising activities. Her house sat back farther from the street than any of the others, and her grandparents had never cut a single tree from their property, so it was difficult to see—and, once you did, the house was a little spooky to kids. One would think this would be the hotspot at Halloween, and she always prepared, but no one ever came.

The buzzing sound came again, and there was no denying it.

Someone was at her door.

Allie placed her glass and her book on the side table and stood. She wandered first to the front living room window and peeked out. A four-door sedan was parked in the drive. Dark in color, blue or black. No markings that suggested it was some sort of salesperson or business vehicle.

Since she couldn't see who had stepped up onto her porch from this window, she moved to the entry hall and had a look through the security viewer on the front door. One man, one woman. Both wore business suits. Both displayed serious facial expressions. Not the typical-looking salespeople. More like police officers or investigators of some sort.

Could be trouble in the neighborhood. A missing child.

Allie took a breath. She really disliked unannounced visits, but she certainly did not want to hinder the search for a criminal or a missing person. "Can I help you?" she asked through the door. Sounded better than "Are you lost?" as an opening.

The man withdrew a small leather case from an interior jacket pocket and opened it for Allie to see through the viewer. The credentials inside identified him as FBI Special Agent Elon Fraser. The photo matched his face, though he'd put on a few pounds since it was taken.

Why on earth would the FBI be calling on her?

"Would you state your business, please?" A reasonable request, in her opinion.

The female spoke up this time while simultaneously flashing her own credentials in front of the viewer. "We are here to speak with Allison Foster," Special Agent Uma Potter explained with visible impatience.

Allie unlocked the door—all three deadbolts. The deadbolts, she remembered now, were her grandfather's idea. He was always certain someone intended to break in and steal his stamp collection or his humidor with his imported cigars. Allie's grandmother would roll her eyes every time he mentioned the idea. Like she had any room to judge. The memories made her smile in spite of the strangers standing on the other side of the door.

She opened the door and surveyed the two once more. "I'm Allison Foster."

Agent Potter gave her a steady perusal as well. "May we come in?"

"Of course." Allie stepped back and opened the door wider. The agents crossed the threshold and waited while she closed and resecured it.

"What are you here to talk about?" Allie looked from one to the other. She had thought Fraser was lead—he was older and had knocked on the door—but maybe she'd been wrong.

"This may take some time," Potter suggested.

Allie nodded. "Follow me." She led the way to the living room, cringed at the sight of her half-finished glass of wine and chocolate bar on the table next to her favorite chair. "Have a seat." She gestured to the sofa.

Fraser waited for his colleague and then Allie to sit before doing the same.

"Ms. Foster," Fraser began, "do you live here alone?"

Not exactly the sort of question a woman who actually did live alone liked to answer when asked by a stranger, but the man was FBI.

"Yes."

"Are there any weapons in the house?" he asked.

"Only my grandfather's BB rifle."

"Your grandmother left you this place?" This from Potter.

Allie nodded slowly. "She did." A frown worked its way across her forehead. "What's this about?" Why would the FBI want to know how she'd come into possession of her property?

Was someone trying to steal her property? She'd heard of this on one of the podcasts she occasionally tuned into. The house was the one thing of real value she owned. Worry needled her.

Potter pulled out her cell phone and tapped the screen. "You're thirty-two years old. Born to Alice and Jerry Foster, who died in an automobile accident when you were four." She glanced up at Allie when she said this as if to gage her reaction.

"That's correct."

"Your mother's parents, Virginia and Gordon Holt,

raised you. You graduated high school right here in Wood-stock and went on to the nursing program at McHenry."

Now Allie was just annoyed. She leaned forward and held up her hands in a stop-sign fashion. "I'm not an-swering any more questions until you tell me what this is about."

Technically, they weren't even questions, just recita-tions of the facts about her life to which she automatically agreed. People did that far too often. Gave away too much information about themselves without even realizing they were confirming details that might haunt them later. Like for someone who might be trying to steal her home.

Stop, Al.

"You're employed by GenCorp," Fraser went on, tak-ing the lead now that Allie had shown her irritation at Potter. "You started with them from their inception, ten years ago."

"Again," Allie said, "I will know what this is about before we continue the conversation."

"Ms. Foster," Potter resumed, "there was an incident at the hospital where you worked which precipitated your leaving the hands-on side of the nursing field and moving to what you do now."

The memory of a patient dying in her arms caused Allie to flinch. She was not going back there. She stood. "I think we're done here."

There was absolutely no reason to talk about that trag-edy. Allie had been investigated by the hospital, the nurs-ing board and the local police. She had been cleared of wrongdoing. It was the doctor in charge of the case who'd made the mistake; Allie had only tried to save the poor woman, and sadly, all her efforts had failed.

"Please—" Fraser eased forward a bit but didn't trouble himself to stand "—bear with us, Ms. Foster."

With visible reluctance, Allie settled into her chair once more. Barely resisted the urge to gulp down the rest of the wine in her glass. Not exactly the sort of move to make with two federal agents staring her down and going over her life history.

"One week ago," Fraser explained, "there was an incident at the hospital where you once worked. A patient was murdered in his room."

Allie drew back, sank deeper into her chair. "I'm sorry to hear that." She allowed a beat to pass. "But what does that have to do with me?"

"Did you see anything about it on the news?" Potter asked.

Finally, a question to actually answer. "I'm afraid not. I never watch the news." She shrugged. "I see the occasional headline pop up when I'm at the computer checking my email, but I rarely follow the link or read whatever commentary accompanies it. I have a weather radio that keeps me informed of the weather, but that's about it really."

The two agents exchanged a glance.

"Can you tell us where you were on Friday, one week ago, from about five in the evening until midnight?"

Allie felt taken aback at the question. "Seriously?"

The way the two looked at her confirmed they were indeed serious.

She shrugged. "Okay. Let me confirm with my phone." She pulled up her calendar app. "I never do anything unless my phone tells me to." She laughed, or attempted to laugh, but the sound came out a little brittle. The agents watching her said nothing. "Okay, here we go. That would have been May 30, and I worked from eight until five, then I had dinner and a shower and started a new book."

When the agents continued staring at her without uttering a word, she looked from one to the other. "*The Great Gatsby.* I've read it like five times, but I sometimes read it again when I haven't decided on anything new."

"We've looked into your lifestyle," Fraser said.

A painful laugh burst out of her before Allie could stop it. Were they joking? "My lifestyle?"

"You don't leave the house often," he explained. "You order most everything online and have it shipped or delivered."

This time, Allie's laugh was more sarcastic. "Since the pandemic, lots of people use online ordering and home delivery. And when you work from home, you don't go out as often." What was the big deal with her shopping habits? Many, after being shut in all that time, just kept living that way. So what?

"Can you tell me the last time you left the house?" Potter inquired.

Allie drew in a deep breath and worked hard to tamp down the irritation that continued to rise. "I don't know. Maybe last month? I think my semiannual dental cleaning was last month. Maybe the fifth. I could check my calendar if you need an exact date."

"With Dr. Rice right here in Woodstock," Potter said.

Okay. Allie braced herself. It was one thing for these two to know her background, but to have been looking into her schedule and her comings and goings? Something was very wrong here.

Before she could say as much, Fraser spoke again. "Ms. Foster, we're here because the victim was part of an ongoing case the Bureau is deeply involved in."

Allie shook her head. "I don't see how my having worked an entire decade ago at the hospital involved has anything to do with your current case."

Again, the two exchanged one of those suspicious glances.

"Just get to the point please." Her frustration refused to stay hidden any longer. She'd had more than enough of this game.

Potter tapped the screen of her cell again, then stood and moved to where Allie sat. "This might give you some clarification."

The screen was open to a video. A woman with brown hair dressed in scrubs paused at room 251. Allie frowned. The woman started into the room but paused long enough to glance first one way and then the other along the corridor, giving the camera a full-on shot of her face.

Allie's attention zoomed in on the image. She studied the face.

Hers.

The woman going into the room was *her.*

Shock funneled inside her. She stared up at Potter. "Why would you have this video? It has to be from at least ten years ago." Allie stared at the frozen image. Her dark brown hair was in a ponytail, the way she'd always worn it—still did. In the video, she wore the required blue scrubs.

"This video," Potter explained, "is from one week ago. That room is where the patient was murdered."

"No. No. No." Allie heart started to pound. She snatched the phone from the agent's hand and watched the video again. "That's me rightly enough. But that could not have been a week ago." She paused the video and tried to zoom in much closer on her face, but it was too blurry to determine if the couple of crow's feet she had developed recently were absent—which, to her way of thinking, would be proof of when this video was actually taken.

She shook her head, passed the phone back to its owner. "I have no idea why you or anyone else would believe that video is only one week old. I haven't been in that hospital since—"

"Your grandmother died at the beginning of the pandemic," Fraser offered.

Allie blinked, a new level of uncertainty settling in. "That's correct." She watched as Potter resumed her seat next to her colleague. "If you know this, then why are you suggesting that video is only a week old?"

"Because it is," Potter stated with complete certainty. "Every second of security footage from that hospital has been scrutinized repeatedly. The clip you watched is the one that occurred outside the victim's room just before he was murdered last Friday. There's another that shows you coming into the hospital that day, but nothing showing you leave."

This was wrong. Allie shook her head, her nerves jangling. "What you're suggesting is impossible."

Fraser moved his head slowly side to side. "I wish it were."

No. Absolutely this had to be some sort of mistake. "But you know I haven't been in that hospital for years. You said so yourself." Worry started to climb up Allie's spine. They were serious. *This* was serious.

"The victim was Thomas Madison."

Allie rolled the name around in her head. "I don't know any Thomas Madison."

This was completely insane. She focused on slowing her breathing. The way her heart thundered she was headed for a panic attack. She did not want to go there in front of these two.

"You may have seen him before." Fraser turned his cell screen toward her. The image displayed there was of a man who appeared to be in his late sixties to early seventies. Gray thinning hair. Light colored eyes. Saggy jowls.

"He doesn't look familiar."

"He worked with your father...before his untimely death."

Allie hesitated. "My father was a research technician at Ledwell..."

At the time—nearly thirty years ago—Ledwell had been the leading-edge AI research facility. Still was. Her father hadn't been a doctor or a scientist, just a tech, but he had been very good at his work. Her grandparents had told Allie stories about how good he was. Most of those in charge at Ledwell had believed him to be far better than any of their academically trained scientists.

"Did you know," Fraser said, "there was an investigation into your parents' accident?"

The transition into her parents' deaths unsettled her further. "I can't say that I knew it growing up, but, looking back, I'm sure that would have been the case. Aren't all accidents, particularly those involving deaths, investigated?"

"Usually, yes," Fraser admitted. "But there was more to your parents' accident. There was some question about whether it was actually an accident."

The wallop that slammed into her chest was Allie's own heart. She gasped, pressed her hand to her chest and fought to calm herself. "I was not aware of this, no. Do you have any evidence of what you're telling me?"

"A couple of reports. The investigation was standard

protocol," Fraser said, "in light of certain anomalies re-lated to the way the accident happened. And no, I don't have all the details, but suffice it to say there were ques-tions. None of which were answered, in my opinion. No matter, the case was closed, and that was the end of it."

Allie got up. She had to move. She started to pace. Didn't care what her guests thought. Why wouldn't her grandparents have told her this?

These two couldn't answer that question any more than she could. What she needed just now was to focus on this moment—this bizarre meeting.

"What does my parents' accident have to do with this Mr. Madison and his murder?"

"We don't know," Potter admitted. "That's what we'd like to find out. Which is why we're here."

Allie paused and aimed a what-the-heck expression at her. "How would I know? I was four years old when they died."

"Right," Potter agreed. "We're hoping your grandpar-ents left notes, letters or some sort of information about the investigation back then that will give us some insight. Apparently the local law enforcement office suffered a fire in the storage area where old case files were kept, so there's nothing on the investigation."

Allie digested this information. "If my grandparents kept anything related to the accident, I am unaware of it." They never talked about the accident. Much was said about her parents, of course. In part to ensure Allie knew how much they had loved her and also to help her remem-ber them. But not much was said about that awful day other than exactly that—what an awful day it was.

"We assumed as much," Fraser said. "We hoped you

might allow us to have a look around the house—unless of course you've purged any and all old papers and files."

"No. I would never do that. This was their home. Their papers and other things are right where they left them." It was a big old rambling house. No need to purge. Not that she would have anyway.

"Then you won't mind if we look for anything useful on finding the truth about what happened to your parents?" This from Potter.

Yes was on the tip of Allie's tongue, but then logic kicked in.

"You came here to question me about a murder." She looked to Fraser. "You have a video—or two—that seem to show me entering the hospital and then the room of the victim on the day of the murder and, I'm assuming, around the time of his death. But then you segued into my parents' accident."

"Because we feel the two are related," Fraser insisted.

"Twenty-eight years apart," she countered.

"Yes," Fraser insisted.

"So you're looking for any thoughts, notes, letters et cetera my grandparents may have kept related to the accident. You're not here to find evidence that would somehow prove your theory about me going into that hospital room and murdering a patient." This was not a question. She already knew the answer.

"Oh," Fraser said with a no-way expression and a wave of his upright palms, "no, we're certainly not looking to railroad anyone. We're here to find the truth."

"So your search warrant will be very specific about what you're looking for," Allie suggested.

"If one is required," Fraser said. "I don't see any need to make it that sort of formal search. Agent Potter and

I could just have a quick, casual look around as long as you're agreeable."

Allie almost laughed out loud. These two clearly thought she was a naïve shut-in. Obviously, they also thought she was a murderer.

Bottom line, she had no idea whatsoever if her parents' accident was anything other than an accident. She also had no clue as to whether their accident was related to this murder at the hospital. And she certainly did not know the victim.

But what she did know was that she wasn't a fool.

Allie paused in her pacing. "Well, thank you for stopping by and giving me so much to consider." She gestured toward the entry hall. "But I believe we're quite finished here."

"You're refusing to cooperate with our investigation," Potter suggested.

Allie smiled at the less-than-subtle pressure technique. "No. I'm just choosing to take advantage of my legal right to say no, not without a warrant. Now, if you'll excuse me, I have a glass of wine and a chocolate bar to finish."

With another of those shared looks, the two federal agents rose from the sofa and walked to the front door. Once they were gone, Allie secured all three deadbolts then went to a window to watch them drive away.

She wondered how long it would be before they were back with a warrant and a team of fellow agents to search the house.

She couldn't think of a reason why she should be worried—there had to be some kind of mistake. But the fact that they had the video showing her in the hospital, supposedly one week ago, entering the room of a man who was murdered, was startling enough to take a moment to think this situation through. As much as she would love to believe it was just some sort of mistake—a woman who looked like her—this was not the case.

This was something very, very wrong.

She had no family attorney. The one who had settled the estate after her grandmother passed away had since passed away himself. She had no friends who were in the legal profession.

In truth, she had lost touch with anyone she had considered a friend years ago. Not due to any falling outs or disagreements. Just because she wasn't much of a socializer, and it was simply easier to focus on work and taking care of her grandmother, and then the pandemic came along.

Life changed.

She leaned against the locked door and racked her brain for anyone who might be able to advise her. Someone she could trust.

Wait. A smile tugged at her lips.

Steve Durham.

He'd joined the police department in Chicago when he graduated high school. She remembered him well. He was a year older, but she'd had a serious crush on him. Not long before her grandmother died, she and Allie had bumped into Steve's grandmother at an appointment at the medical center. The two had discussed being widows and having grandchildren. Allie remembered Mrs. Durham talking about how Steve had left the police department after only a year, deciding instead to go to university. Then he'd gone on to law school. He'd been hired right away by some fancy, as she called it, private investigations agency in Chicago. What was the name of it?

Oh yeah. *The Colby Agency.*

Chapter Two

"I realize it's late," Victoria Colby-Camp, the head of the agency said. "But—" she gazed at her most trusted associates around the long conference table "—we have to make a decision before any of us go home for the weekend."

Steve Durham smiled. Victoria was never one to mince words. Nor was her granddaughter, Jamie. She'd come on board just six months ago, and already she was doing a stellar job. Jamie was so much like her grandmother. It was clear to Steve and everyone at the agency how very proud Victoria was to have Jamie at her side.

Tonight's after-hours meeting was about the two open investigator slots. The agency's clientele list continued to grow, and actually they needed to add at least five. But it was difficult to find the caliber of investigator this agency employed. The Colby's longstanding reputation was one of the reasons Steve had decided to become a part of the agency.

Lucky for him he had started right out of law school. Victoria had personally sought him out and offered him a position. She'd explained that one of his professors at

Northwestern had called to say Victoria needed to have a look at Steve. He'd been damned surprised and extremely humbled by the recommendation. According to Victoria, his background in law enforcement made him uniquely qualified as an attorney, in her opinion.

Steve was grateful. He had five years at this agency so far and hoped for many, many more. It was an honor, really, to work with Victoria.

He scanned the faces around him. Working with people like Ian Michaels, Nicole Reed Michaels, Simon Ruhl and Victoria's son, Jim, was an opportunity he'd never expected. He glanced at the young woman seated next to Victoria. Jamie held her own with the very finest the agency had to offer. She had proven very quickly that she deserved to be the leader of the agency—in training of course. She represented the next generation of this agency and represented it well. And then there was Lucas Camp— Victoria's husband—who was a legend in his own right. Just knowing him was a privilege.

Steve genuinely appreciated that his work here was not confined to the typical corporate or financial legal business of being an attorney. He was more like one of the investigators, but his job was to advise and steer any investigator who might find themselves in a tight situation, legally speaking, out of trouble. It was the perfect combination of practicing law and putting it into action in the field.

"I'm in agreement," Ian Michaels spoke up. "Jamie and I have interviewed both candidates, and we're more than pleased with what we've seen."

"The two are a perfect fit," Jamie agreed with a nod of her blond head. She smiled. "I wish we could find two or three others so qualified."

Good news for the two candidates,· for sure. Those gathered around the table weren't impressed by anything less than outstanding performances.

Jim Colby spoke up next. "On separate occasions, I was accompanied in the field for a day, first with Chance Rader and then with Billie Jagger. I was also impressed with their bearing and communication skills. I say let's do it."

There was a whole barrage of other requirements for agency investigators that included self-defense skills and the use of weapons. Every investigator was as fully trained as any police officer on the street. From time to time, a case required those skills, and the Colby Agency never let down a client.

All looked to Steve then. "I have thoroughly reviewed the backgrounds of both candidates, and I'm fully satisfied we should move forward with offers of employment."

"Very well." Victoria smiled. "Jamie, if you will relay the good news so that our new investigators don't have to spend their weekends in suspense."

Jamie stood. "I'll make those calls now."

Victoria rose from the head of the table. "And I will get home to the celebration dinner Lucas is preparing."

Victoria and Lucas were celebrating the birth of another grandchild. Lucas's son, Slade, and his wife, Maggie, had just brought home a new baby. This was number three for the couple and a bit of a surprise since their others were fourteen and twelve. Life had a way of tossing out those little surprises. Fortunately, in this case, all were pleased.

By the time Steve closed up his office and headed for the elevators in the lobby, everyone else was gone. They all had families waiting at home. Busy weekends ahead, no doubt.

He tapped the call button and waited for a car to return from the lobby.

Behind him the agency phone started to ring. He glanced at his watch. Half past seven. Since the office was closed, the call would go to the answering service, where it would be appropriately routed.

Indeed, the ringing stopped, so he stayed put at the elevator doors, waiting. When the ringing began once more, he couldn't ignore it. He crossed to the receptionist's desk and picked up the handset.

"The Colby Agency."

The silence on the other end suggested the caller had either given up and disconnected or that the call had gone directly to the answering service after that second ring.

Oh well, he had tried.

"Hello."

He'd had the handset headed toward its cradle and scarcely heard the faint word. "This is the Colby Agency." He rested the handset against his ear once more.

"I know it's late." The voice was a woman's. She released a breath. "I really thought you'd be closed, and I'd be able to leave a message."

His initial thought was to ask if she preferred that he direct her call to voicemail. Some matters were of such a private nature that a client might wish to say them to the voicemail rather than to a person, a stranger, first.

Before he could suggest as much, she spoke again. "I'm glad you're not." There was a hesitation, then, "I think I might be in trouble."

Her confidence was building, and his curiosity was

doing the same. "Would you like to make an appointment to come into the office?"

"Well, I'm… I'm actually looking for Steve Durham. Can I leave a message for him?"

Interesting. "No need. You've got him. This is Steve."

The woman lapsed into silence once more.

"How can I help?" he prodded. The elevator chimed, and the doors slid open. Since he was on the office phone, he couldn't go for it. He'd call another when this conversation was finished. There was no reason to rush. Unlike his colleagues, he had no one waiting at home.

"You might not remember me," she said, the hesitation back. "My name is Allie Foster."

Recognition flared instantly. A smile spread across his face. "Allie, yes, I remember you. Of course I do. If not for your brilliant mind, I might never have managed precal." Wow. Talk about a blast from the past.

The damned class had given him nightmares. At the time, he'd told himself it didn't matter because he wasn't going to college anyway, but his mother had insisted he take all the right classes in case he changed his mind later.

His mother was a very smart lady.

"Yes. That was a tough semester, but you got the swing of it by second semester."

The smile in her voice told him she had relaxed a bit. "Are you in Chicago now?" How long had it been? Sixteen years? Fifteen for sure.

"No. I'm… I'm still in Woodstock living in my grandparents' house." A strained laugh followed. "I'm sorry to call so late, but I'm not sure this can wait."

"I understand." He checked his watch. "I could be there in just over an hour. Why don't I drive out? If you haven't had dinner already, I could pick up takeout and we'll catch up. Figure out the situation."

The whole idea came out in such a rush, he felt walloped by the force of it. But, for some strange reason, he sensed it was the right thing to do. Maybe it was the hint of desperation in her tone or just the fact that she reminded him of the good old days. Whatever the case, he wanted to help. Her return to silence suggested he'd maybe pushed a little with the idea.

"Or we could wait for you to come to the office on Monday. I'm good with either plan, Allie."

"I'm not sure waiting is a good idea. If you could come now...that would be great." She exhaled a big breath. "But that's so much trouble. Are you sure you don't mind?"

"I do not mind at all. In fact, I insist." His lips twitched with another memory. Her grandfather showing him how to change a tire. Steve had borrowed his father's little project car—a two-seat convertible—without permission that hot summer day to impress a girl who wasn't impressed with him at all. Never was. He'd gotten a flat right in front of the Foster home. Allie had watched the tire-changing session from the window and then the porch, but she'd been too shy to come out and say hello. The next year, his pre-cal teacher suggested Allie as a tutor. It had taken some time, but she had eventually learned to relax in his presence.

"Good," she said with relief. "Great, I mean. Do you remember the address?"

"I do. You up for Chinese, or would you prefer Mexican?"

"You choose."

"Chinese it is. See you in an hour or so."

"Okay. Thanks, Steve. Really, thank you so much."

"No thanks necessary. I owe you, Allie Foster."

He placed the handset back in its cradle and called another elevator car. This late the traffic wouldn't be so bad.

There was a great Chinese place on the way.

He smiled. *Allie Foster.* How many times had he thought of her over the years? Several. Why had he never called or dropped by to see her? Asked her to dinner? He should have kept up with her. She was a really nice person.

This was the perfect opportunity for him to make it up to her for all the times she or her family had helped him out.

Foster Residence
Ridgeland Avenue, 8:50 p.m.

STEVE SENT ALLIE a text to let her know he'd arrived at her street. As he navigated his SUV into the driveway, she switched on the exterior lights. The porch and yard area close to the house brightened as if the sun had suddenly risen and shone only on that spot. The over-the-top exterior lighting reminded him of something else about Allie's family. His mother had insisted that after the accident—meaning the car crash that took the life of the Holts' daughter and son-in-law, Allie's parents—the family hadn't been the same. It was as if they had feared that something would happen to their granddaughter—their only surviving family member. They'd hovered over her, keeping extra close tabs on her every move.

Maybe that was part of the reason she'd been so painfully shy. She was the quietest kid he'd known.

But then she was the only one he'd known who had lost both parents before she was old enough to go to school.

It was a tough break.

She was also brilliant and pretty and very sweet.

But that was a long time ago, he reminded himself. Things and people changed. She might not be that same wallflower anymore.

He shut off the engine, grabbed the bags of food from the passenger seat and climbed out. He would know soon enough. By the time he was on the porch, the door opened—but not before he heard at least three locks disengaging.

Maybe she had her reasons. Either way, no judgment.

"You're here."

The genuine surprise in her voice and her expression made him wonder if she'd been let down a lot by friends who promised to drop by or do her some favor.

"Food, too." He held up the bags. The smell of lo mein and fried rice had haunted him all the way here.

She ushered him inside and to the dining room, which was actually a part of the kitchen. A typical L-shape allowed the smaller part, the dining room, to flow directly into the living room. It was one of those houses with a larger second floor. The best he recalled there was nothing on the first floor beyond the main living space. All the bedrooms were up one floor. No basement, if he remembered correctly. He glanced around. Definitely not much had changed about the place.

"This is like déjà vu," he said as he settled the bags on the table.

She laughed a soft sound. "I really haven't upgraded anything, just replaced whatever gave out. Decor isn't my thing."

He nodded his approval. "I like it. Your grandmother had great taste."

Allie glanced around. "She wasn't like the other grandmothers, that's for sure."

The very sixties-seventies vibe was evidence of that
statement. In his opinion, the couple had been the coolest
grandparents ever. Steve had always seen Virginia Holt
and her husband, Gordon, as old hippies who probably
smoked pot in the basement and were saving the wild par-
ties for when Allie would eventually be away at college.

Except, according to Steve's mother, Allie never went
away to college. She'd stayed right here in Woodstock. In
this very house. Allie hadn't changed much, either. Still
had that long brown hair trapped in a ponytail. He vividly
remembered how her brown eyes lit up when she laughed.
He would wager she had no idea how gorgeous she was.
With her tee that sported flowers and I'd Rather Be in the
Garden along with well-worn jeans, she looked eighteen
instead of thirty-two. Her grandmother had dressed the
same way and always looked far younger than the other
grandmothers, even with her long gray hair that she'd always worn in a braid.

"Wine or beer?" Allie asked. "I usually drink wine,
but I had beer delivered after we talked."

Home delivery almost any time of the day or night was
an amazing thing. "I'm good with whichever is handy."

Once they were settled with plates filled and drinks
handy, Steve suggested, "Why don't you start at the beginning and tell me what's going on."

After her call, there hadn't been an opportunity for
him to do any sort of research or to call anyone from
the agency who could do a bit for him this evening. Ul-
timately, he'd decided to wait and hear what she had to
say first.

Walking into the situation cold wasn't a big deal, he'd
known her most of his life.

He watched her face as she spoke, going over the visit

from the two federal agents. Allie really looked so much like the young girl he'd known in high school with her fresh, makeup-free face and ponytail. Unlike him, she didn't seem to have aged at all. Her voice still had that lyrical rhythm to it. He liked the sound of it. And when she got going with a story, her face came to life, emotions on full display. Her memory appeared to be outstanding as well. Her account of the conversation held with the agents was very detailed.

"I did a little looking into the murder," she said as she poked at her rice, the momentum of her retelling slowing down. "Thomas Madison was a big deal—a partner at Ledwell. You probably don't remember, but that's where my father worked when he died."

"Ledwell." Steve nodded. "I'm familiar with the company. Fortune 500. Hot investment even all these years later. They've held their own in a very competitive marketplace."

"I found that surprising as well. Usually someone else comes along who is a little better, but no one has been able to get ahead of Ledwell in the AI race. This murder has sent shockwaves through the industry and Wall Street, which I suspect is part of why the FBI is involved. Fraser and Potter said Madison was part of an ongoing case, so my guess is their case had something to do with the research currently being conducted at Ledwell or something from recent years."

Steve chewed thoughtfully for a moment. "Ledwell is the one that won that huge government AI contract just last year."

"You're right, and I'm sure you've heard about the various issues coming to light. There's a lot of controversy in the AI arena right now. According to Google, Ledwell is pushing back on any new restrictive legislation. They've basically had free reign until recently, and they're not taking the changes well."

Steve reached for his cell, tapped the notes icon and started a list. "We'll put AI R&D at the top of our list of motives for the situation—not necessarily for the man's murder but for whatever is happening behind the scenes right now that may have impacted in some way the event or events that culminated in his death."

Allie set her fork down, and her shoulders sagged with the way she let go a weary breath. "I'm so glad I found you and that you came."

He grinned. "Of course. It's what friends do."

Maybe friends was a stretch considering the time gap, but she no doubt understood his intent.

They ate in silence for a while. Steve watched her. She ate with considerably more enthusiasm now that her trouble was on the table. It wasn't every day someone was visited by the FBI and accused of the murder of a man she didn't know in a place where she hadn't been in years. She had every right to be upset and defensive. He appreciated that she had enough faith in him to sound reasonably relaxed and open in spite of the concerns likely reeling in her mind.

Steve pushed his plate aside and settled his forearms on the table. She did the same, her gaze on his, searching. The pulse at the base of her throat fluttered again. She was visibly braced for his conclusions.

"I don't practice criminal law or really any other at this time," he explained. "I primarily counsel and advise the agency on operational matters. I can represent you if that's what you want."

"Yes!" Her relief was palpable. "Please. Thank God."

He smiled. "Our first step is to learn what the FBI believes and what the two agents working the case wish to prove with their visit to you. Are you their only suspect? Is closing the case quickly more important than digging around for other possibilities? I want to meet with Agents Fraser and Potter and get a feel for where they are with all this. Once we discover what precisely they want from you and what they hope to gain by pushing for the search of your property, we'll have a better handle on just how bad the situation is for you."

Her shoulders sagged again. "The woman in the video is me. I'm reasonably confident it is," she admitted. "But I was not there last week or any other day in the past five years."

"Videos can be doctored—made to show what the editor wants others to see."

She nodded. "I'm aware, and I considered that might be the case."

"There's also the possibility the video is from when you worked at the hospital. The room number may have been altered for the purpose of making it fit the narrative they wanted to present. The big question in my mind is why are they so convinced it's real? The Bureau has the ability to determine if the video has been altered. I'm guessing that not showing that card gives them leverage—something to use to get what they want."

"It must have been altered. There's just no other explanation." She bit her lip as if considering whether to say the rest of what was on her mind.

"Do you have other thoughts about how that happened?"

She shook her head no. "I was thinking that it might be a good idea to go through the house. Maybe see if I can find anything at all related to Ledwell or this Thomas

Madison. But I was worried it would make me look guilty if they showed up with a warrant and I'm in the middle of tearing the place apart."

"It's your home," he pointed out. "You can search it any way at any time you choose."

She looked away a moment, the heavier worries seeming to catch up with her once more. "I don't understand why this is happening." She set her gaze on his. "I've lived right here my whole life. I don't know this victim. I don't see how someone could have picked me out and decided I would be the person they used to get away with murder."

"Obviously it's someone who needs an alibi and is aware that you worked at the hospital before and that there was a connection—your father's employment with Ledwell. If he or she is involved with AI, chances are we're looking at someone with above average intelligence. Perhaps even a fixer or…" He shrugged, almost hated to bring this up. "Or maybe an assassin whose skill set includes cleaning up after him or herself. You would be part of that clean up."

"My God, I hadn't even considered anything along those lines."

"I hope that's not the case," he offered, "but we need to consider all possibilities."

"I was four years old when my parents died," she said, frustrated. "I barely remember them. Why would I go after someone all these years later who may or may not have been a part of whatever was being investigated after the accident? I had no idea there was an investigation beyond the usual kind related to automobile accidents. My grandparents never told me." She turned up her hands. "I am utterly in the dark about all this."

"It's possible they didn't know," he ventured, though

he thought that was unlikely. "Do you know if there was a settlement related to the accident? Was anyone else involved?"

"No. It was a single-car accident chalked up to a mechanical failure. At least, that's what I was told."

He studied her a long moment. "Why did you leave the hospital—when you were a nurse there?"

She exhaled a weary breath. "I loved helping people. It felt good and important—like what I was meant to do. Sadly, there are those in the field who don't always do good or even close to good. I saw that firsthand right from the beginning." She shook her head. "Long story short, when someone died, I couldn't pretend I didn't know why it happened. When I went to the administrator about it, I was made to look like the bad guy. At that point, I had two options. Get fired or quit. I chose the latter and decided to find a different way to help."

"You're saying someone in the hospital's administration gave you an ultimatum." Not good for the current situation. It could be seen as motive.

"Not in a straightforward way, but basically that was what the situation boiled down to."

"But you never pursued legal action? Never went back and raised hell? Nothing like that?"

She shook her head. "Nope. Just did what I wanted to do in a different way."

He supposed that was what he was doing, practicing law in a different way than the typical attorney. Nothing wrong with achieving your goal using a different path.

"It's late," he said, considering that at minimum it was an hour's drive home. "I should get going. But I'll be back in the morning, and we'll nail down more of our strategy,

and who knows?" He smiled. "Maybe we'll do a little digging around here if you're up for it."

"I am definitely up for whatever you think we should
do." She drew in a big breath. "Thank you so much for
coming all this way. We should probably discuss what
your fees are."

The look of hope and gratitude on her face was more
than enough payment. Part of what had made him want
to go into the legal field was to be able to help those who
were being unjustly persecuted.

This was a perfect example—at least based on what
he had heard and seen so far.

"You don't need to worry about any fees."

Before she could argue, he insisted on helping to clean
up, and then she walked him to the door. Even with the
strange story of her being suspected of murder, he had to
admit he had enjoyed seeing her again.

The doorbell abruptly buzzed.

Startled, Allie looked from the door to him. Shook her
head. "No clue."

He checked the viewfinder and discovered two suits
and a row of personnel dressed in CSI garb lined up on
her porch. He didn't have to wonder who the suits were.
Federal agents.

"They're back." He turned to Allie. "And they obviously have a warrant. Don't answer any questions. In fact,
don't say a word. Let me handle this."

She nodded her understanding.

Since it had only been a few hours since the agents
questioned Allie, it seemed out of the ordinary that the
pair was back so soon with a warrant. Warrants generally
took time. Whenever an investigation was being pushed
fast and hard, there was either an imminent danger of

some sort or someone powerful who wanted this done ASAP pushing for a rapid turnaround.

He opened the door to the two agents and their party. Steve didn't have enough information to hazard a guess one way or the other, but what he understood without doubt was the situation was not in Allie's best interest.

This was a clear and present threat to her.

Chapter Three

Allie watched as the group of agents filed out of her house for the last time.

Outrage did not begin to describe how this felt. These people had combed through her house, through all her things, literally all night. She had been forced to stay outside. Steve had tried to talk her into going to a hotel, but she'd refused, so she'd ended up in his SUV for the duration.

As her attorney, he had been allowed to stay and to watch the proceedings inside the house. He'd come outside to check on her more times than she could remember. Actually, she remembered every single one. His blond hair was darker now, more a light brown. And his eyes were the most calming shade of blue.

Stop, Al. He was here to help with legal issues not fulfill her fantasies.

She straightened in the passenger seat, now that it appeared to be over, finally. Maybe she could put this behind her and life would go back to normal.

She blinked. Had her life ever been normal?

Allie pushed the thought away. She wasn't going there right now.

Steve stood on the sidewalk and watched the crew load up and drive away before returning to where she waited. She reached for the door handle. All she wanted to do was get in her bed and sleep…put this nightmare out of her head. Maybe check her email. Social media wasn't her thing. She was probably the only person her age on the planet who had no social media account.

He opened the driver's side door and slid behind the steering wheel. "You up for Red's?"

A frown furrowed across her brow. How could he sound so chipper? Then again, he wasn't the one whose life was suddenly upside-down. Besides, he likely experienced situations like this in his work. It was probably par for the course on any given day at the agency. While her life was a continual routine of bed at ten, up at six, work and then repeat. There was something to be said for routine…but mostly her life was dull.

Allie took a breath. Red's was a local diner that opened at five every morning for breakfast. The good, old-fashioned kind of food like her grandmother used to prepare. As if that wasn't incentive enough, when was the last time a handsome man had invited her anywhere?

Her stomach rumbled, but she shook her head. "I'm really not hungry. I'd like to go inside and—"

"Let's have breakfast first." He started the engine and turned the vehicle around.

She plowed her fingers through her hair, imagining how utterly awful she looked. The ponytail had to go hours ago. "It must be bad if you don't want me to go in there before having sustenance."

"They put things back where they found them, just not quite as neatly."

She groaned. "Yay. I might as well do a little late spring cleaning." That would make her vacation even better. How much more exciting could her life get? *Woo-hoo!*

Considering she was under suspicion for murder, maybe that might not be a good question to ask herself. In this case, excitement was a little overrated.

He drove to Red's, which was only minutes from her house. She ordered delivery from them a few times each month. It was her grandparents' favorite dining spot. Maybe because Red Shepherd, the owner, was an aging hippie just as they had been. Allie couldn't help smiling. She missed them so much.

She covertly glanced at the driver. Her grandmother had always said Steve was a good boy. Like his father, she'd said. Allie had seen photos of her mother as a teenager with Steve's father. Her grandmother had given the impression that she'd wished those two had ended up together.

Steve glanced at her. "You must be thinking about the past." He guided the SUV into a parking slot. "The present certainly wouldn't prompt a smile like that one."

She touched her lips. Hadn't realized she'd been smiling. "I was thinking about my mother."

He smiled back at her. "You look like her. Exactly like her."

"Everyone always says that." And the family photo albums confirmed it.

He hopped out of the vehicle and hurried around to her door before she could rally the energy to open it.

"Not that I really remember her," he said as she

emerged. "But my mom has lots of photos of family gatherings that included your parents."

"I've seen a few in my grandmother's albums." Allie smiled. She and her grandparents hadn't gone to very many gatherings with neighbors after her parents were gone. Things had changed after that.

The bell over the door jingled as they opened it and walked inside.

"Looks like we're the first customers today," Steve noted.

The smell of bacon drifting from the kitchen had Allie's stomach rumbling again. "I think I changed my mind. I'm starving."

He grinned. "Good. We need to load up on carbs and sugar and then deal with this thing."

There was something to be said for his strategy. Allie just wasn't exactly sure what it was quite yet. She was, however, immensely grateful to have someone to help her navigate this nightmare.

They took a booth near the back since the diner would likely fill quickly on a Saturday morning. A waitress materialized, carafe of fresh coffee in hand. She filled the waiting mugs and took their order.

When she disappeared back into the kitchen, Allie said, "Tell me about your work at the Colby Agency." It would be nice to think about something else for a little while.

He nodded. "The Colby Agency is the best in the business. Truly the best. Victoria is an incredible force, as is the entire staff. It's a privilege to be a part of the team. I'm happy there."

"Do you investigate cases?" She pressed a hand to her chest. "Like this mess I find myself in?"

"Actually—" he took a sip of coffee then set his mug

aside "—I don't do the investigating, but I get involved when there are potential issues that fall into the legal category. I do a lot of advising on cases with the investigators. My time with Chicago PD helped with that aspect of my work. It's one of the reasons Victoria was interested in interviewing me when I finished law school."

Allie studied him for a moment. "I always got the impression that college was not your thing. I mean, you never talked about it. What made you change your mind and go to college and then to law school? That's a serious commitment for someone who wasn't big on the idea of university life."

He laughed. "I think my experience is a little like your own. I very much enjoyed my work on the force, but I felt there was more I could do from this perspective, so I changed gears."

The waitress arrived with their orders, and they dug in. Apparently, Allie really had been starving. She'd barely eaten last night. The food he'd brought had been great, but her appetite had been absent. The whole situation with the murder and those FBI agents had been overwhelming.

It still was, but her body was adjusting to this new stressor.

After the need for food had been satisfied for the most part, she lifted her gaze to his. "Tell me about what happened inside my house. You spoke to Fraser and Potter, I assume."

He nodded and set his fork aside. "Both are convinced the woman in the video is you."

Her hopes sank.

"That said," he went on, "both are fully aware the video could have been created from one taken when you were employed at the hospital. They aren't convinced that you are the person who murdered Mr. Madison, but the only evidence they have points to you. For the most part, I believe they feel whatever happened is somehow connected to you, and this is the leverage they have, so they're using it."

Allie shook her head. "Why would I kill a man I don't even know?"

"Exactly. They're aware."

"Did they go into the case that involved Madison—the one they were working prior to his death?"

"They did not, but it is related to Ledwell. I was able to get that out of Fraser. This has something to do with the company, and your father's connection—however old— to that company lends credence to your possible involvement. Which is why they wanted to see whatever was in the house and on your computer."

Allie's heart sank, joining the hopes that had fallen around her feet. "They took my computer."

He nodded. "And your laptop and cell phone and tablet."

The thought shook her. How would she do anything without one or the other of those devices? Her whole life was electronic.

She sagged deeper in the booth.

"They will return all your belongings," he promised. "The only question is when. For now, we will get you another phone and a laptop if you need one for work."

She shrugged. "I'm on vacation until a week from Monday. I can live without my laptop. But not my phone."

He grinned. "Who could?"

"Well, well, if it ain't my favorite goddaughter."

The boom of Red Shepherd's voice turned every head in the diner, and the place had pretty much filled up at this point. Allie wasn't so much concerned about anyone recognizing her. She rarely left the house. Anyone who had known her growing up wouldn't remember her now. Likely wouldn't even recognize her.

Along with social media, she hadn't bothered to cultivate friends. Her life was all about work. But there were other people—ones who had known her parents and grandparents—who still remembered her. There were a few at work she considered friends, sort of. She knew their online work profiles, their voices.

But that didn't really fit the definition of a friend.

Allie worked up a smile. She wasn't actually Red's goddaughter, but he had claimed the title when she was a kid. "Great to see you, Red."

He slid into the booth next to her. He studied Steve a moment. "You're Martha's boy, aren't you?"

"Yes, sir."

Red looked from one to the other. "Good to see folks from the old neighborhood still coming around."

Allie decided to take a chance. She was here. She might as well. "Red, do you remember much about my father?"

He made a puffing sound. "Are you kidding? Course I do. He stole the heart of the prettiest girl in Woodstock." He grinned. "Lots of guys around here never forgave him."

Allie laughed. "I wish I remembered more."

Red nodded, his face somber. "What happened was a terrible thing."

"Do you remember anything about his work at Ledwell?" Steve asked.

Red studied him for a long moment before answering. Allie's nerves went on edge.

"His work was not something he talked about. It wasn't

allowed. No one talked about what went on in that place. Still don't. But, to answer your question in a roundabout way, there was a problem at Ledwell back then," he said with a covert glance around their booth. "There was tension. Your grandparents," Red went on, his gaze shifting to Allie, "were concerned about what he was getting into. He wouldn't talk about it, but they suspected it was bad business."

"Do you believe my father was involved in some illegal activity?" Allie's grandmother had certainly never said anything of the sort.

"No." Red swung his head in a firm negative. "It was something bad though. Your mother wanted him to leave the company, but he was afraid he'd be blackballed and wouldn't be able to get another job, so he stuck it out."

"The Holts never mentioned anything specific," Steve nudged the older man, "as to what the issue was?"

Red gave another shake of his head. "No, but we all knew there was funny business at that company. Getting into all kinds of research that was going to come back to haunt anyone involved, I suspect. All our concerns got played off, and we were called paranoid and what-have-you, but we were right. It's all coming out now." He leaned forward. "All that AI business is going to be the end of us, you mark my word."

There were those with that opinion, for sure. Allie wasn't sure where she stood on the matter.

"Do you think my parents were afraid?" All these years, she had believed it was a simple car crash that took their lives. Bad luck. Wrong place, wrong time. But maybe that wasn't true.

"I know your grandparents were." He nodded, his face grave. "And after the accident, Virginia and Gordon went to the police, to the FBI—to anyone who might listen. But no one would. They were labeled crazy…overwrought with grief. Didn't matter. They knew that accident was no accident. We all knew it."

For a moment, Allie couldn't speak. There had been questions. She always sensed that, even as a child. But no one had ever uttered those words out loud.

No accident?

"Do you have any evidence?" Steve pressed. "Did the Holts ever talk about any real evidence?"

To Allie's knowledge, they certainly never had, but she kept quiet…mostly because she wasn't sure what to say.

Red smirked. "What do you think?"

Allie held up her hands. "I don't understand why I have no memory of this…this nightmare you're describing."

Red smiled sadly. "I'm sorry. I get carried away when I allow myself to think about it. The reason you don't remember, I guess, is because a year after the accident your grandmother put her foot down and called it enough. She and Gordon were fighting a losing battle, and they knew it. Nothing they had done had gotten the investigation beyond some BS mechanical malfunction conclusion. Virginia decided there was nothing she could do about what happened to her precious daughter and her husband, but she could be a part of what became of you. *You* were more important. They decided they would put the past behind them and focus on taking care of you. On giving you the best life possible."

Allie didn't doubt this for one second. Her grandparents had always been overprotective and had over planned everything for her. They offered to send her to the best college, but she turned down all options except the one that kept her close to home. After all they'd done for her, she couldn't bring herself to abandon them. Maybe deep down she had always known something wasn't right with what happened to her parents.

All this time, that vague notion had simmered inside her…and now it was out. She didn't know exactly how to feel.

"I think," Allie began, "what you're telling me is someone murdered my parents, in all likelihood, because of something my father knew or did in his work. My grandparents let it go in an effort to protect me."

Red held her gaze for a long moment. "That's exactly what I'm telling you."

She wanted to jump up and demand to know where the cameras were and what reality television show had decided to make her the subject of its newest episode. But she understood that wasn't the case. Her emotions were spinning. One moment she was angry, the next terrified and then…just numb. But…this was real. All these years, the things she had believed about her family were stories made to keep her safe…to keep her happy and not digging around.

Yet now…somehow…something had gone wrong. A glitch in the stream of life had occurred, and now she was being drawn back into this no matter that she had no idea what this was.

Red shook his head again. "I've said too much."

"No." She managed an appreciative smile for him. "It's way past time I learned the truth. You did the right thing."

"But your grandparents worked so hard to protect you, and I just undid two-and-a-half decades of their efforts." The emotion shining in his eyes warned that he was dead serious.

Allie wasn't exactly sure what to say to make him feel better.

"Unfortunately, Mr. Shepherd," Steve said, letting her off the hook, "someone else has already opened that door, and now we need all the help we can get to figure out who and why. What you've done is give us a starting place for finding answers."

The older man's relief was so visibly overwhelming Allie thought he might actually cry.

"I'll give you something else," he said with another of those covert glances around. "Find Jesus. He can give you way more information."

"Jesus?" Steve and Allie said in unison with equal surprise.

"Jesus Rivero." Red winked. "He was a hotshot reporter back then. Almost got himself killed a dozen times trying to get the story, and he always did…until that accident. Talk to Jesus—if you can find him. He'll know how to help."

Steve tried to pay the tab, but Red insisted it was on the house. Allie gave him a hug.

All they had to do now was find Jesus.

Chapter Four

Wonder Lake, Illinois
Rivero Residence
Lake Shore Drive, 8:00 a.m.

Steve parked in the small driveway. Allie surveyed the street. She'd never had reason to be in the area. The properties here were miles beyond her price range. Surprisingly, the house that was their destination sat practically in the street, as did most along this stretch of the neighborhood. It was also much smaller than she had expected for such a pricy area. In all probability, the reason was because the houses on this private lake did their showing off out back, not in front. Though she couldn't recall ever having been here, she had seen the property online. She'd looked it up on the way here. This side of the house was for access from the street, while the other side was the one with the view and the jagged and plummeting landscape down to the water.

A white, vintage Land Rover Defender sat as close to the house as was possible without the rear bumper contacting the stone and wood facade. She hoped the vehicle being there meant the owner was home. Although, considering the dust and tree sap clinging to the surface, it may have been sitting exactly where it was for a good long while. Maybe he had another vehicle and a garage somewhere she couldn't see.

On the drive over, she had used Steve's phone to do some research on Jesus Rivero. Thirty years ago, he had been the hottest reporter in the Chicago market. He'd even been slated for his own primetime show, but then something happened and he just dropped off the face of the earth.

Red had passed along that part, but he hadn't known where Rivero had disappeared to. There was nothing on the net about his whereabouts either. Recently, the former bigtime reporter had been spotted in the Chicago area, but he hadn't moved back to his penthouse apartment there. Instead, he'd sold it for one dollar to the family who had been leasing it for all those years. According to the online county records, and Allie had checked several counties surrounding Chicago, he'd bought this house on Wonder Lake around that same time, just three months ago.

The man, various articles had purported, was a recluse, given that he was rarely seen in public. Allie couldn't ignore the fact that, in that regard, their lives were a little alike. Though she had never considered herself an actual recluse. Not in the truest definition of the word anyway. But maybe that was what she was. She didn't socialize with friends. Didn't do social media. Had no dating prospects. Rarely left the house since the pandemic. Maybe her friends from her childhood and school, as well as those from her time working at the hospital, all thought she had dropped off the face of the earth too.

During those years she'd taken care of her grandmother, there had been no time to worry about anything else other than work. It was an around-the-clock gig. Not for one second did she regret the choice. Even after her grandmother died, the pandemic had made it far too easy to stick with the status quo. Stay home and shop via delivery services.

Something similar may have happened to Rivero. Maybe his disappearance was no mystery at all, just a tragic life event.

"Shall we go to the door?"

Allie jerked at the sound of Steve's voice. "Sorry, I was lost in…the past again."

"You need sleep. When we're done here, I should take you home and let you get some sleep."

Did that mean he was leaving? The idea sent fear spiraling through her.

Rather than express that fear, she nodded as she reached for the door handle. "I really appreciate you taking so much time with me. I can't believe it's evolved into such a nightmare. I'm sure you have to get back to Chicago."

She didn't even want to imagine what he thought of her. Poor, pathetic Allie. Giving herself a mental kick, she put aside the idea. There was no time for self-pity right now. She was in trouble, and she needed his help—whatever his motive for going above and beyond.

"I do need to make a quick run to the city," he agreed, "to grab a few things, but I'll be back. This is far from over, Allie. I'm not leaving until this is done—at least, not as long as you want me here."

Her spirits lifted as high as possible, bearing in mind she really was exhausted. "Thank you. I'm not sure I know the right words to adequately express how grateful I am." She opened the door and climbed out before embarrassing herself by going further overboard with the relief and appreciation.

He joined her in front of the SUV, and they walked side by side to the door of the house. Steve rang the bell. No answer. Two more rings were required before there was a response. Allie's pulse had pounded harder with each passing second. At this rate, she was going to hyperventilate before they even spoke to the man.

"If you have a package," the muffled voice echoed over the speaker next to the doorbell, "just leave it at the door."

Steve glanced at Allie. "Mr. Rivero, this is Steve Durham of the Colby Agency in Chicago. I need a moment of your time, sir."

"Who is *she*?" the voice demanded.

Allie had just noticed the camera tucked into the soffit over their heads. Well, of course he had cameras. She had considered adding a few herself but never got around to it. Maybe she should.

"Allie Foster," she answered. "You may have known my father, Jerry Foster. He was a technician at Ledwell before being killed in a car crash."

The silence went on and on. Her stomach twisted into knots. Was his hesitation because he did know her father? Or because she had mentioned Ledwell?

"You were working on a big story related to Ledwell," Steve said, obviously hoping to prompt a response other than silence. "We just want to ask you a few questions about what happened back then."

"I can't help you," the disembodied voice muttered.

Desperation rose sharply in Allie. Red was convinced this man knew something, which meant Allie needed to talk to him. "Thomas Madison is dead. Murdered. They think I killed him, and I don't even know him. I believe his murder is somehow related to what happened to my parents. Please, Mr. Rivero, I really need your help."

"What you need," the man inside the house snapped, "is to go home and forget anything you think you know because I promise you, you don't know *anything*. You don't want to know anything. Not if you want to stay alive."

Allie's jaw dropped. Was this guy for real? "I can't fight an enemy I don't recognize," she argued. The idea might be a bit over the top, but that was exactly how she felt just now. "At least help me determine what I'm up against here."

"That's all we're asking for," Steve tossed in, "just a few minutes of your time."

"You're up against a brick wall," the voice said. "I can't help you."

"You mean," Allie countered, furious now, "you won't help me."

The distinct click of the man inside turning off the intercom link confirmed her conclusion.

"I guess he doesn't want to talk," Steve suggested.

"Maybe Red was wrong about him."

They walked back to the SUV and drove away from the disappointment. Allie abruptly felt lost and utterly out of energy. How had this happened? It made no sense whatsoever. If her grandparents had known there was some big, dangerous mystery, why hadn't they warned her?

She had to assume they either hadn't known or expected that as long as she knew nothing about it, the trouble would never come to her.

If that was the case, they had been wrong. She refused to believe they would purposely have left her open to trouble.

"We can always try again," Steve offered. "We'll do as much research as we can without his help, and then we'll hit him up again. Meanwhile, I have some sources I can reach out to."

Allie couldn't remember when she'd felt so frustrated. Didn't reporters like talking about their work? It was possible Rivero was just a burned-out old man who didn't want to admit that he had no stories left in him. Or that the one he'd been pursuing before his disappearance had turned out to be nothing of relevance.

Bottom line, there was pretty much nothing she could do about Jesus Rivero's decision. But there was something that would not wait any longer.

"I need a phone."

"That's our next stop," Steve assured her. "We have to get you connected to the world again."

She wasn't so sure she'd ever really been connected. Maybe that was her mistake. How did a person provide an alibi for murder or any other crime without a witness—someone who could vouch for them. Allie had no one. No friends—at least none with which she communicated, outside the few at work who only knew her voice. Her alibi was that she had been at home. Alone. Since she rarely left the house, her neighbors certainly couldn't provide an alibi.

In the eyes of the two FBI agents, that was no alibi at all. An evening with F. Scott Fitzgerald didn't count.

Foster Residence
Ridgeland Avenue, 11:30 a.m.

NOT ONLY DID Allie buy a new phone, but she also splurged on a new laptop as well. The one the FBI agents had taken was four years old already. It was time. Besides, who knew when she would get her devices back.

At her front door, since Steve still had the key, he unlocked and opened the door. She held her breath, dreading what she would find inside. He'd warned her that things were a bit disorganized.

She set down her bag of new goodies and wandered through the downstairs rooms. Not so bad, she decided. Nothing a little straightening wouldn't take care of.

"Did they take anything with them—besides my devices?" She turned to the man following along behind her. "I saw some of the agents carrying boxes."

"They took a number of files from your office and a few photo albums. Not that much really. What any investigator leaves a scene with is always telling. They obviously didn't find the stash of goods or files they had hoped to discover. For now, we can consider that good news."

Allie surveyed the entry hall then glanced up the stairs. "I keep trying to wrap my head around what's happening, and it's just not working. It feels like a bad dream. Like I should wake up any time now, and it will all be over."

"Completely understandable." He nodded. "I'm heading to my place for clothes and a few other things I need. I'll be back in a couple hours. Get some sleep. We'll start breaking this down when I return."

"Thanks. I really appreciate this, Steve."

He gave her a quick hug. "This will be just a bad memory before you know it."

She had her doubts, but she could hope. The surge of warmth she felt with his arms around her was certainly something she would not soon forget.

Foolish, Al. You definitely need a life.

When he'd gone, she secured the three deadbolts and climbed the stairs to see the damage there. Her office was on the second floor, so she would charge her new phone

Alibi for Murder

and laptop and get them activated as well. The sooner she could do something constructive, the better.

He had suggested she sleep, but Allie wasn't sure she would be doing that again anytime soon.

At least not until she understood what was happening here.

She stood at the door to her grandparents' room and felt sick at how the agents had pilfered through their things. But it wasn't until she reached her parents' bedroom that she wanted to throw something. They had taken the room apart, one piece at a time. The furnishings and the things in those furnishings hadn't been touched since the car crash. But those damned federal agents had come into the house and gone through their belongings with no care for their sentimental value to Allie. The items in this room were all she had left of her parents.

Once she'd calmed down and set her new devices to charge, she headed for the shower. Losing herself in a long hot shower would be a relief right now.

Her mind wouldn't slow down even with the hot water sluicing over her skin. She tried to relax, to find that Zen place that would allow her to think clearly and focus on the details of what was happening. So she closed her eyes and thought of the man who'd spent the last several hours with her.

She hadn't seen him in what? Fifteen years? He was still just as handsome as she remembered. Maybe more so. And smart. Really smart and kind. Back in high school, he was one of the nice guys while others his age had been busy showing off. Not Steve.

A bit of time was required and a whole lot of hot water, but the effort to focus on anything but the FBI and their murder accusations eventually started to work. Her shoulders and neck and then the rest of her stopped fighting the need to relax.

When she turned off the water and stepped out into the cool air, she felt much better. She brushed her teeth, dressed in her favorite sweats and climbed into her bed. She hadn't meant to sleep, only to relax, but suddenly she just couldn't keep her eyes open any longer.

Thoughts of that hug she and Steve had shared followed her into sleep.

A SOUND POKED at Allie. She told her eyes to open, but they refused. She was so tired. She needed to sleep just a little while longer.

Then the sound crept deeper into her consciousness.

A buzzing...like the doorbell.

Why would anyone be at her door? She never had visitors. Only deliveries.

But the buzz came again, and her eyes fluttered open this time.

Someone was at her door. She sat up. Her head felt fuzzy, and she had to think a moment before she could find her way back to the here and now.

Murder.

The video of her going into a patient's room.

Steve Durham. The Colby Agency.

The FBI was investigating her.

For an instant, she wanted to drop back onto the pillows and close her eyes tightly to block this crazy reality. Instead, she climbed out of the bed and stumbled out of her room and along the hall. Steve was probably back. She finger combed her hair on the way down the stairs. With a puff of breath into her hand, she tried to gage if it was fit for exposure to anyone beyond herself. Vaguely she remembered adding toothpaste to her toothbrush last night.

Another insistent buzz. She was almost at the door.

She reached for the first of the deadbolts but stopped herself. She needed to be sure who was on the other side, especially now.

Going on tiptoe, she checked the viewfinder in the door and smiled. Steve stood on her porch, a leather overnight bag in one hand and a briefcase in the other.

What time was it?

As she unlocked the door, she checked the grandfather clock just behind her. Three thirty. She'd slept better than two hours, closer to three.

She opened the door and smiled, hoping she didn't look a hot mess but fairly confident she did. "You're back."

"I am and I have some news."

As soon as he was across the threshold, she closed and locked the door. "Potter and Fraser made a mistake, and it's not me they're looking for?" she asked hopefully.

"Not quite that, but additional information that can help us with finding our way out of this mess perhaps just a little more quickly."

"I'll take any kind of break at this point."

Amazing what a difference twenty-four hours can make. A mere twenty-four hours ago, she had been working her final shift before vacation and had no idea trouble was headed her way. Blissful ignorance. She should have appreciated it more.

"Did you manage to get some sleep?" He dropped his bag onto the bench next to the door but hung on to the briefcase.

"Oddly enough, I did."

"You up for coffee or tea?"

Coffee sounded amazing as a matter of fact. "I can put on a pot while you tell me what you discovered." She led the way to the kitchen.

Once she had filled the reservoir and added grounds to the filter, he kicked off his update. "Your father was one of six staff members closely involved in the SILO project."

Allie set the machine to brew. "Never heard of it." Surely if the project had been significant, she would have heard something about it in all these years. Artificial intelligence, or AI, was certainly in the news frequently enough. Even more so lately.

"You wouldn't have," he explained. "The project carried the highest security clearance requirement the US government uses."

Well, okay then. "Tell me about the project."

She leaned against the counter, the smell of coffee filling the room. Inside, she dared to smile. He had this way of making her feel totally comfortable—as if it hadn't been a decade and a half since they'd seen each other. As if they had been friends all this time.

"Special Intelligence Learning Operative," he explained. "They were working on the creation of AI operatives who could go under deep cover and learn everything there was to know about the enemy. Ones that could anticipate the movements of the enemy based on their knowledge of said enemy. All without risking human life."

Okay, they had just entered the twilight zone.

"Robots who look and behave like humans well enough to infiltrate the enemy?" Maybe not a total surprise. She supposed that particular goal had been an ongoing effort since the inception of AI.

"Yes," he confirmed. "Except this project hoped to take it further than ever before—for the timeframe we're talking about. That said, the really important part as far as you're concerned is the fact this project was primarily funded by the CIA and the military. Not your usual government scientific research."

This gave Allie pause. "So, we're talking about spooks and secret agents."

"In all likelihood, yes. My contact confirmed there were some issues related to where this project was headed, and it was eventually disbanded—or so that was the claim."

Nothing he'd told her sounded particularly troubling. Government projects were started and then stopped all the time. Issues cropped up, et cetera. "What makes the cessation of the project different than any of the others we hear about all the time?"

There were plenty of examples of hidden research that came out years or decades later. In some ways, she understood that the technology race had to be secretive. There were far too many in the world who would use it for all the wrong reasons.

"No idea about what makes this one different—as of yet," he admitted. "But what we do know is that five of the six employees closely involved in the project died suddenly and tragically within just a few weeks or months of the shutdown."

A shock wave shuddered through Allie. "Then my parents' accident was likely no accident." On some level, she didn't want to know this…she wanted to let the past be just what it was…the *past*. She wanted to go on with her life believing the loss was merely another of life's tragedies, and her grandparents had picked up the slack.

Except it was too late for that. She'd already heard the words.

"I don't see how we can continue to call it an accident," Steve agreed. "But there's still a lot to discover before we can confirm a conclusion along those lines."

"Who was the lone survivor?" She already knew the answer, but she needed him to confirm her suspicion.

"Thomas Madison."

The corroboration quaked through her. She busied her hands with pouring the coffee. She didn't use cream, and based on breakfast this morning, Steve didn't either.

"Why was Madison allowed to live until just recently?" She passed a mug of steaming brew to him. "Seems like a loose thread to me."

"That's the part that doesn't fit neatly into what I'm hearing about this project so far. I have people digging. For now, that's the best we can do."

She cradled her mug of coffee and wondered what the hell any of this meant. "Potter and Fraser may not want to wait about making an arrest." The truth was, she could be sitting in a jail cell by dark or by morning. There was just no way to know which way this was going to go.

"Fraser has requested a meeting at ten on Monday morning." Steve shrugged. "If an arrest was imminent, I'm not sure there would be a reason for the meeting."

She wanted to feel relieved, but then again, all the delay suggested was that their people would spend all weekend going through the things they had taken and trying to find something relevant to the murder so that they could charge her.

Allie exiled the negative thought and sipped her coffee. Better to be optimistic and to see this upcoming meeting as a good thing.

"Until then," Steve said, "we'll search this house again just to be sure they didn't miss anything, and we're going to visit Mr. Rivero again. Maybe two or three times until he will talk to us or files a complaint with local law enforcement."

That all sounded like a good plan. She set her mug aside. But there might be one glitch. She should have broached the subject already, but things had been a little out of control until now.

"I know you said I shouldn't worry about fees, but we really need to talk about your retainer." She had some money saved. She had her grandparents' insurance funds as well. Whatever the Colby Agency fee, she should be able to handle it. But if she couldn't that was a whole other nightmare.

He looked her straight in the eye and said, "There will be no retainer or fee of any sort."

"Wait." She frowned, shook her head. "No. You're here representing me and a lot more. You need to be paid your usual fee. I'm sure your agency will expect me to be treated like any other client." No way was she having him do this for free.

"No." He shook his head. "I'm doing this for a friend. I've already taken some of my vacation time so I can be right here working on your case for as long as it takes. And no worries. I'll still have all the support I need just one phone call away. Although we'll be spending most of our time here or in the field in pursuit of information, I reserved myself a room at the Baymont."

"No." Him getting a room at a hotel was ridiculous. "Look, there's plenty of space right here. If you insist on this no fee thing, the least I can do is put you up and feed you."

He laughed. "That would be the most efficient choice—if you're sure."

"I am positive."

"Then I'm staying here."

Allie relaxed then. She had faith in Steve. He'd proven he could handle those agents, and he had all sorts of resources if even half of what she'd read about the Colby Agency was true.

In all honesty, she still felt unsettled by the idea of not being a paying client of the agency. But that was his choice, and she had to get right with it. Because the one thing she understood with complete certainty was that this man was likely the only way she was getting out of this nightmare free of a murder charge.

Chapter Five

Foster Residence
Ridgeland Avenue, 5:30 p.m.

Over the course of the past two hours, they had searched the house again. Allie had taken the bedrooms; Steve focused on the common areas. She had picked through every single article of clothing...every little thing.

She supposed this was why by the time she reached her parents' room, which she saved for last, Steve had finished with the rest of the house.

"You searched your office as well?" Standing in the doorway, he surveyed the room that had belonged to Jerry and Alice Foster.

"I did." He'd suggested a thorough search of her office when they first started. Even though she had been the one to set up all the furniture and the other odds and ends of her workspace, she'd done so while her grandparents were still alive. One or the other could have hidden something there later. In some distant part of her brain, she'd considered as much before Steve mentioned the possibility, but she hadn't really wanted to believe either of her grandparents would have hidden anything from her. The very idea was ludicrous.

This whole situation was ludicrous. She eyed the man standing in that doorway...except for him. He was the one thing keeping her grounded amid this ever-escalating madness.

Pushing aside the worrisome thoughts, she considered that whatever she had believed about the past and her grandparents, here she was in a total state of uncertainty about both. Clearly many things had been hidden from her.

Whatever else she believed at this point, Allie was completely certain her grandparents only did whatever they did to protect her. Red had said as much, but she hadn't really needed his confirmation. Her grandparents had loved her. She had absolutely no question about that.

"Let's go at this room," Steve suggested, surveying the twelve-by-about-fourteen space that had been her parents' bedroom, "from a different angle."

Allie was ready for just about anything as long as it helped solve this mystery. "Tell me what you mean."

"Let's consider that your parents hid something specific for reasons other than what Red suggested—that they were protecting you."

She made a face. "I'm confused. I thought we were looking for anything they'd hidden for whatever reason."

He shrugged. "We've been looking for anything hidden, yes. But what if this was some sort of insurance for them? At the time it was hidden, they may not have realized that you might be in danger as well. Any move or decision a person makes is always motivated by some necessity. Each move or decision is different based on the immediacy and/or the necessity involved."

Allie thought maybe she got it now, though she wasn't entirely sure. "You're saying that they may have hidden something differently if it was related to a more imme-

diate need the two of them had versus some future need
I might have."

He smiled. "Precisely."

Made sense.

They started with the ceiling. There were no ventila-
tion registers in the ceiling, and only one light fixture
which was actually a ceiling fan. Steve rounded up a ladder and checked the tops of the blades to ensure nothing
was tucked there. He examined the main part of the fixture as well. Nothing but dust.

While he examined the curtains and blinds on the windows, Allie studied the walls. She looked behind framed
items hanging there. She scrutinized every single crack
in the plaster for possible openings. She removed the cov-
ers from electrical outlets, including the light switch, to
ensure nothing was hidden in those either.

Piece by piece, they moved the furniture away from
the wall and inspected the backside, the underside—
including those of the drawers. It wasn't until they pulled
the bed from the wall that they found a possible *former*
hiding place.

"This—" Steve pointed to a spot in the wood on the
back of the headboard "—is a place that was once covered.
Maybe by a label of some sort or by something taped there."

The spot wasn't very large. About the size of a post-
card. She traced it, felt a sticky residue. She nodded. "It
may have been nothing more than a manufacturer's label.
But there was something stuck there."

He pointed to an actual label on the opposite side. "This
is larger. Why have two labels on the same piece of furniture when the others by the same manufacturer and in
the same set we've already examined do not?"

He was right. The bedroom suite's matching dresser

and side tables only had one label each, always posted on the back of the item.

"Whatever was hidden here is gone now." It felt very much like they were grasping at straws. Playing a guessing game. What if? Maybe this...

He smiled, though the expression looked as weary as she felt. "We are reaching. And it's frustrating. But we're trying, and until one of my resources comes through, it's the best we can do."

"Beats sitting around waiting for the other shoe to drop." Allie would openly admit that she was one of those people who needed to be focused on something most all the time.

"Always," he agreed.

Then they checked the floor. Each board of the hardwood was touched and examined for looseness and the possibility of being removed, along with the floor registers and the duct work leading up to those registers. Still nothing.

They had moved everything. Looked in, on and under everything.

Allie lay on her back on the floor. There was nowhere else to look.

Her gaze shifted from the bedroom door to the closet door. They had examined by hand each of the doors, smoothing their palms over the surfaces. The closet door was different from the main one leading into the bedroom. Not original, she decided. The door that led in and out of the room was like all the rest in the house. Paneled insets with wood stiles and rails. The usual type found in homes of this age and style. The closet door was similar in that it looked the same, but it wasn't. Allie rolled onto her hands and knees and made her way to it. The inset panels weren't really panels with stiles and rails. Each side of the door was molded to resemble a paneled door to create a "fake" paneled door.

Had the original door been replaced because it was damaged?

Steve crouched next to her. "This door is different. Newer."

She sighed. "Still no place to hide anything as far as I can tell."

"Except—" his gaze narrowed "—some newer doors, like this one, are called hollow core. They're mostly hollow on the inside with just a little wood here and there for holding the whole thing together." He ran his fingers along the edge, between the floor and the bottom of the door. Then he stood, went for the ladder they'd been using and stationed it next to the door. He climbed up and inspected the top.

"Anything?"

The smile that spread across his face answered the question. "There's wood, maybe an inch or so thick, typically across the top and bottom for stability. But a section has been removed here." He tapped the top. "Very carefully removed."

"Do you see anything in there?" Her pulse started to beat faster. It was about time they got a break.

Using the forefingers of both hands, he probed the space, eventually pulling out a plastic bag that had been taped inside. "Not your typical hiding place," he noted, "but certainly effective."

Apparently nothing about her parents had been typical.

He stepped down from the ladder and passed her the plastic slide bag. Allie settled on the bed and opened it. A white envelope folded over photographs was all that it contained.

Heart racing at the possibilities, she shuffled through the photographs. There were three couples total, all three in one photo, one or two in each of the others. Her parents and two other couples she didn't recognize. The photos appeared to have been taken during outings or get-togethers of some sort. Their clothing was casual....smiles on their faces.

"Let me see that again." Steve pointed to one of the photos she held.

She passed it to him. It was a photograph of a couple she didn't recognize. She stared at the remaining three. Why would these be hidden so carefully? What was the relevance of the photos? Location? The people? There were no objects in the setting that appeared wrong or out of place. Were they playing some private couples' sex game they feared these photos would point to? Allie didn't see how. They all looked completely innocent to her.

"This—" Steve tapped the man in the photo "—guy looks familiar."

Allie leaned closer and studied the face. "Wait. You're right. I think maybe..."

She got to her feet. "I need my laptop."

Steve was right behind her as she hurried to her office. She opened her laptop and pulled up the most recent file she'd sent to her email. She'd saved what she was able to find on Thomas Madison there.

The row of images were from Madison's career at Ledwell over the years. She pointed to the oldest photo, where he appeared the youngest. "That's him."

The man in the photos—in two of the photos found in her parents' hidden place—was a younger Thomas Madison.

Her gaze settled on Steve's. "He and my parents were friends."

Steve pointed to the photo. "Is the woman his wife? A girlfriend?"

"His wife died three years ago." She selected another

photo in the file. The woman pictured there certainly looked very much like the one in the photo. Older, of course. "It could be her."

"What have you found about her?" He shifted his attention to her laptop.

"Her name was Jane. Maiden name Talbert. Died three years ago." She shrugged. "That's it."

Another dead end.

"Do a search on Talbert. See if she has any surviving family."

A few clicks of the keys and lines of search results spilled onto the screen. "Here we go." Allie selected the one for Jane Talbert in Woodstock, which helped to narrow the results significantly considering the size of her little town.

Steve leaned toward the screen, a hand braced on her desk, while he read over her shoulder. She wished she could claim not to be affected by his nearness—this certainly wasn't the time—but she was undeniably affected. Warmth spread through her body. He made her feel… safe…alive.

"Father is deceased," he said, his jaw so close to her cheek. "No mention of her mother."

Allie forced herself to focus on the screen. She opened another tab and tapped on the obituary for Jane Talbert Madison listed on the new webpage. "No children. The obit mentions no surviving family at all other than her husband, Thomas Madison." Allie frowned. "But her mother's name isn't mentioned. Just the names of her father and siblings, who died before her. I suppose it could have been an oversight."

"Let's have a look at any property owned by Jane or her father," Steve suggested.

Allie opened another tab and went to the official county

property search site. A few taps of the keys later and she had just one listing on screen. The property was different from the one listed as Thomas Madison's home. A look into transfers and Allie figured out it was the property owned by the wife's father that she had inherited more than thirty years ago. Again, no mention of her mother.

"She inherited this property about five years before my parents died," Allie noticed, saying as much out loud.

"Which means your parents may have visited the Madisons there. You may have as well."

"Only one way to find out." Allie closed her laptop. "Let's have a look."

"You'd make a great investigator," Steve said as he followed her out of her office.

Allie laughed. "I may have been guided toward where I needed to look by someone with considerable experience."

He chuckled. "We all start somewhere."

She couldn't help thinking again how lucky she was to have him helping her out with this total mystery that had descended upon her life.

She just hoped that, however this ended, it wouldn't be the conclusion of this rekindled friendship.

If she was really lucky it would be just the beginning.

She almost laughed out loud. *Wishful thinking, Al.*

Talbert/Madison Residence
Justen Road
McHenry, Illinois, 7:00 p.m.

THE PROPERTY WAS around half an hour away from Allie's home.

But it was not what she had expected at all. The twenty acres had been listed on the county map, but the house was totally different from what she'd envisioned. It was a massive barn that had been renovated into a home. Those sorts of renovations had become popular in recent years, but it seemed unexpected three decades back. Maybe the Madisons had been ahead of their time where home design was concerned. Or perhaps Mr. Talbert had done the renovations before giving it to his daughter.

As they parked, Allie noted a good many other details. The place was a little rundown. Slightly overgrown. It looked as if no one had been here in years. Made sense, she supposed, since Madison's wife had been dead for three years. Maybe he hadn't found the time or the desire to see after the property. They had moved to their most recent residence twenty-nine years ago.

Steve parked. "You want to get out? We still have some daylight left."

Allie nodded. They were here. Might as well have a look around.

She almost smiled at the idea. Though she rarely left the house, he somehow managed to have her ready for all sorts of adventures. Just went to show that you could do whatever necessary when thrust into a situation like this one.

Maybe all she'd needed this whole time to come out of her protective shell was someone to be adventurous with. Or perhaps the more likely scenario was that deep down she wanted to impress him. She did not want this man to see her as a shut-in or a recluse…or a nobody.

What better way to prove the rumors untrue than to be adventurous?

The woods were thick all around the yard that had been carved from it. The house sat smack in the middle of that clearing, lending even more privacy to the structure since only the driveway made any sort of path through the thick circle of trees. Based on the aerial view she'd seen on the county listing, more woods and some pastureland rolled out behind the yard and the house.

They emerged from the SUV and walked to the front door. Sunlight filtered through the massive windows along the side of the house as they passed, allowing her to see inside. There was furniture. Did that mean someone lived here? Maybe. A ring of the doorbell and a knock on the door garnered no response. A repeat of both resulted in the same.

A cautious walk around back found more needed maintenance for the home and landscape and no sign of human habitation. How strange that the house had been seemingly abandoned with all its contents. Didn't people usually take their things or sell them when moving?

Allie studied the outside of the house. She suddenly felt jittery, and she had no idea why…until she discovered the large pavilion—a gazebo-like structure detached from the back of the house and almost hidden in the trees. The fading sunlight trickled through the vines and shady branches that grew over it. Something about the way the faint light dappled through and formed shapes tugged at her memory.

"I know this place."

The words she whispered were so soft she doubted Steve had heard her, but she was lost in a memory she couldn't quite capture. Some elusive slip of something she recognized but couldn't grab on to.

Allie walked around, studying the wood structure with all its vines and overgrown shrubs. The wood was failing in places, screaming for attention.

"You believe you've been here before?" Steve appeared next to her.

"I don't know…but it feels like I have." She turned to him. "You know that feeling of having been somewhere, but you can't quite place it? Maybe I saw it in photos. If my parents had been here, then there were likely photos. My grandmother said my mother loved taking photos."

"Then let's take our time." He assessed the yard that spilled beyond the trees to a fenced pasture. "We'll walk the grounds and then come back to the house and have a look through any window we can reach."

She was moving before he finished speaking, her mind searching for a place to land. A place that some part of her recognized.

At one time, the property had been beautifully land-scaped. The long-neglected shrubs were not the sort to be found growing wild. Many boasted scattered blooms that spoke of their beauty. Others were just beginning to bud. Stacks of stones and boulders guided them into other little venues designed for outdoor use. Tables and benches dotted the landscape, most badly in need of maintenance.

In the center of it all was a massive swimming pool that sat half full of dark green water. The pool had an hourglass shape. Allie could imagine that at one time it had been gorgeous. A path that meandered from the pool toward the woods circled a large three-tiered fountain. Around the base of the fountain were rose bushes. Some struggled to bloom, but most were overgrown with weeds, the leaves speckled with holes from whatever insect had decided to feed on them. So sad.

She wandered back to the house. The windows on the first floor didn't prompt any additional feelings of recognition. But she peered at length through each one nonetheless. It was almost dark by the time she felt she had seen anything potentially relevant to the fleeting memory that tugged at her.

"You need to see anything else?" Steve's patience seemed endless.

Her own patience had run out, but she took one last lingering look around. "I think I've seen all I need to. Whatever I feel like I remember, I can't quite capture it."

"You want to grab dinner at a drive-through on the way back to your house?"

She paused at the front of his SUV. "Works for me."

She hadn't placed a delivery order for groceries in a while. The offerings in her fridge and pantry were likely sparse.

IT WAS DARK when they reached Woodstock. She insisted that Steve choose the fast food. Burgers and fries were his choice, and she was so thankful. She could use all those carbs right now. She wouldn't have selected a burger joint for fear of insulting his culinary senses. He looked so fit. She suspected he ate only the healthiest items on a menu. It was good to know he was an occasional let's-eat-the-greasy-stuff guy.

It was also nice to know he wasn't totally perfect. No matter that he seemed completely perfect to her.

"What does your girlfriend think of you staying with an old friend for a few days?" She suspected he wasn't married since there was no ring or mention of a wife, but surely there was someone.

If she hadn't been completely exhausted and floating in anticipation from the scent of those fries wafting from the bag on the console between them, she might have done a better job of filtering herself.

Too late to regret the question now.

He glanced at her. "I do not have a girlfriend or a wife." He exhaled an audible breath as if saying so saddened him somehow. "I've been so focused on the agency for the past few years there really hasn't been a lot of time for a social life."

"A totally overused excuse," she told him straight up, feeling bolder now, maybe because she was almost home and he was…*single*. "Try again."

He glanced at her, grinned. "I've dated. Just haven't found the right one."

"Is that because you're too picky?" This was also a seriously overused excuse.

He laughed then. "Maybe. How about you? Are you too picky or just too busy?"

No one to blame but herself for creating the corner into which he'd just backed her. "I'm not sure I've even considered a social life. Not since college anyway." She shrugged, thinking back to the last time she actually thought about dating. "I had lunch with someone a couple of times before I left the hospital. Not really anything since. I guess I'm just a loner." She laughed. "Wow. That's pretty sad. Almost ten years with no tangible social life."

"We're busy," he repeated as he navigated into her driveway. "You had your grandmother to take care of. I was finishing law school."

"That's such a lie," she suggested with a soft laugh. "Personally, I think it's easier to believe I'm too busy than to put myself out there and risk… I don't know. Rejection? Dissatisfaction? Total emotional gutting?"

He shot her a look. "You may have a point." He parked and shut off the engine. "You're what? Thirty-two? I'm thirty-three. Going forward, we should make ourselves a priority. I'm game if you are."

"All right, Dr. Phil. I can do that."

They both had a good laugh at that one. Laughter was good. She, for one, had needed a decent laugh.

Steve unlocked the door and went inside first to ensure there was nothing amiss. Allie kind of enjoyed the chivalry. It was a pleasant change from doing everything herself. He was a nice guy. Even nicer now, she decided.

Again, she considered how fortunate she was that they had reconnected, in spite of the reason.

While he unbagged their dinner, she went to the bookcase where her grandmother had kept all the family photo albums. That memory she couldn't quite grab from the gray matter deep in her head had nudged her all the way home.

She sat down on the floor and picked up first one and then the next album, flipping through the pages looking for something she couldn't name.

Then she paused, her fingers on the edge of a page she'd been ready to turn. "Found it!"

Steve joined her on the floor. She moved the album to where he could see the photos as well. There were several pages of two of the couples, the Madisons and her parents, all photographed at the Madison/Talbert property.

"Wow," she said, "it was really beautiful back then. I knew I'd seen it somewhere."

"But why hide the photos we found in that closet door and not these?" Steve studied the photos. "It had to be about the third couple—the mystery couple—or surely these photos would have been hidden as well."

He was right. That third couple was the only different aspect in the photos. Made sense.

Allie turned to him. "We need to figure out who the third couple is, and maybe we'll learn some part of the story."

"You took the words right out of my mouth."

She stared at his lips, thought of how he would taste.

"But first—" he hitched his head toward the dining room "—we need to eat those cold burgers and fries."

"Oh." She grimaced at herself for staring at his lips. "Sorry about that. I got completely caught up in figuring out where I'd seen the place before and lost all track of time."

He stood and offered his hand to assist her in getting up. "The wine will help the fries go down easier."

Allie grabbed his hand and pulled herself up. She glanced at the table. He'd found her stash and opened a new bottle of red. The flush of embarrassment crept over her cheeks.

"You know I really don't drink that much. I just believe in having plenty on hand in case of an emergency."

"It's always best to be prepared." He grinned at her. "I have my own stash exactly like that at home."

Her heart took an extra beat. Preparation was important. She'd always believed so. She really liked that he did too.

But after years of self-imposed seclusion, she wasn't sure it was possible to be adequately prepared for this man.

Panic nudged at her...all the other thoughts she wanted to ignore closing in.

Or being suspected of murder.

Chapter Six

Sunday, June 8
Foster Residence
Ridgeland Avenue
Woodstock, 8:00 a.m.

Allie finished off her toast. It wasn't such a great breakfast, but when she had suggested it based on the offerings available, Steve claimed cheese toast was one of his favorites. The toast and coffee had done the trick for her. She wasn't a huge breakfast fan anyway. Her typical days consisted of brunch and dinner. As for the menu, like this morning, it was generally driven by whatever was in the house. Or something she had delivered if she was feeling the urge.

She really needed to get better organized. Her grandmother had always taken care of running the kitchen. Until she was no longer physically able to do so, she had insisted that it was her domain. Allie could be in charge of all the rest, but she was to leave the kitchen to her grandmother. It was great until her grandmother could no longer handle the job. Then Allie had just felt guilty for being inept at kitchen duties. Her culinary skills still left much to be desired.

During her grandmother's illness, Allie had tried to carry on with the usual menu items. Her grandmother had many cookbooks with dog-eared pages. But once she was gone, sandwiches and microwave meals became the norm.

Maybe Steve was right. Allie should focus a little more on herself.

Working at home made the concept more difficult, in her opinion. It was far easier to pull on a pair of sweats and tuck her hair into a ponytail and not care. Who would see her? No one. And the whole cooking for one was not as simple or as stress-free as it sounded.

Steve glanced at his cell, answered an incoming call and wandered out of the kitchen. Allie cleared away the paper plates—another bad habit of hers—and wiped off the table.

Who wanted to wash dishes for one? There was a dishwasher, but it would take days to load it with enough items to feel it wasn't wasteful to turn it on.

Just another excuse.

She had to admit it had been nice to fall asleep last night knowing someone else was in the house. Even nicer to wake up and share coffee and toast with a really smart, handsome man who…

Okay, slow down, Al.

She shook off the random thoughts and rinsed their coffee mugs, then placed them on the drainer.

Steve came back to the door, his call obviously completed. "That was my mother. She insists we come to dinner. You okay with that?"

For one moment, fear paralyzed her. What would she wear? What would Mrs. Durham think of her now? Would she believe Allie capable of murder? The story hadn't been in the news yet as far as she knew, which surprised her, but still people talked in small towns. His mother lived here. She would no doubt hear all the rumors and gossip.

Allie faked a smile and nodded with pretend enthusiasm. "Sure."

"We'll take the photo of the mystery couple," he suggested, completely undaunted by the idea. "Mom or Dad might know who they are."

"Good idea." He'd sent a copy to one of his colleagues. Hopefully between that person and the Durhams they would learn the identity of the mystery couple. The fact that the photos with that couple were hidden seemed to imply some sort of secret.

But who knew if it was related to anything. It could be a waste of time.

Allie breathed a little easier about having dinner with Steve's family. All she had to do was focus on the issue at hand. Everything else would work out.

"You ready?" he asked when she lingered at the sink.

She pushed aside the worries and shifted her attention to where it belonged. "Absolutely."

They were taking another field trip—this one to Thomas Madison's most recent home. Maybe they would notice something the federal agents had not. Like some clue that pointed to the truth.

Probably wishful thinking.

Madison Residence
Hamilton Road
Woodstock, 9:30 a.m.

THE MADISON HOME was neglected like the Madison/Talbert property. Not quite as overgrown but utterly run-down with lots of deferred maintenance.

The place was well off the beaten path. The home stood a good distance back from the road, at least a mile, amid eighty acres of wooded land, according to the county property records. Obviously it was an expansive property. The nearest house on either side of the road was quite a distance away, but there was one directly across the road from the long driveway.

Also like the other property, the house was an older one. Not a refurbished barn this time but one of those boxy modern styles with too many angles and lots of windows so popular in the 70s and 80s. Since it sat where the property sloped downward on one side, there appeared to be a walk-out basement level.

It was unusually warm today. Allie was grateful for the shade of the generous number of trees around the house. She and Steve climbed the steps to the front stoop, which was too narrow to officially be called a porch, and rang the bell. The light above the door was on as if waiting for the owner to return. She put her hands on either side of her eyes and peered through the glass sidelight next to the double set of doors.

A foyer led directly into a large, open-concept room with a soaring ceiling. Wood beams, wood floors. Exactly what one would expect in a home of this style and era. It was furnished the same way, with some modern-looking pieces.

No one came to the door since the owner was lying on a stainless-steel slab at the morgue. He had no family to take over the property, much less to claim him or to see to his final arrangements.

Infinitely sad.

Allie suddenly realized she was in that same boat. No next of kin. No close friends. All her work associates were nothing more than voices on radio waves bouncing off cell towers.

She drew back mentally, banished the sad thought. Not exactly reaffirming.

Steve walked down the steps and started around the corner of the house, and Allie followed. In addition to the garage that was part of the house structure, there was a detached garage. Beyond that was what might be a barn. Not big and tall like the older ones, but something more modern and space conscious with a lower roof line.

The two of them peered through each first-floor window just as they had at the other house. The more they looked, the more obvious it was that the house had been thoroughly searched. Drawers either weren't quite closed all the way or sat askew. Items atop those same pieces of furniture sat in no particular arrangement. Pillows and cushions on the sofa and chairs were not fully tucked into place. All appeared *out* of place. As she had thought, on the one end where the ground sloped, there was a lower level that opened to the outside with windows and French doors. The shades or blinds were drawn tight over those windows as well as the doors.

There was nothing about the property that felt familiar to Allie. Nothing at all.

"I don't recall any of the photos having been taken here," Steve mentioned.

"I was just thinking the same thing. Most were in public places, at our house or at the house on Justen. This is such a large property I'm surprised they didn't do hikes or picnics or something here." She supposed they could have and for whatever reason hadn't taken photos that day. It was a very attractive property, discounting the needed maintenance, particularly if one was a nature lover.

"Let's check out the detached garage and barn."

Allie followed him, still wondering why no photos had been taken here. It really was the perfect setting. They had moved here an entire year before her parents died, so it wasn't because it had been unavailable to them at the time.

The detached garage was unlocked. Although they had no official business here and certainly no legal right, Allie needed to look. Before she could say as much, Steve opened the door and they went inside. The electricity was still on, so the flip of a switch provided the necessary light to survey the interior. Inside were the tools found in most home workshops. Those for making repairs around the house as well as a few for vehicle maintenance. Nothing that personalized the space. No photos or calendars or brand memorabilia hanging on the walls.

The low roof-line barn was their next destination. Inside were stalls for horses but no indication horses had ever been there. The floors were clean. No leftover animal droppings or deteriorating straw or hay. No gear for riding horses in the tack room. The barn looked as if it had never been used for any purpose.

From there, they returned to the house.

"I guess we've seen all there is to see," Steve commented, "unless we opt to do a little breaking and entering. Bearing in mind the Bureau and the police have both likely searched the place already, I don't see any reason to cross that line. Yet, anyway."

Allie glanced around. "I'm with you on that one. I suppose we could have a look under some of these flowerpots. They don't appear to have been disturbed recently, and there's a lot of them." She smiled with a memory. "My grandmother used to hide a house key under one.

Sometimes when we played games, she would hide clues under the flowerpots."

This was probably a task that really would prove a waste of time, but why not give it a shot?

Steve considered her at length, his expression serious. "I really do like the way you think, ma'am. Your grandmother too."

She laughed. "You can let me know if you still believe that when we're done and all the spiders who probably call those pots home have shown their displeasure."

The clay and ceramic pots were in various sizes and styles as well as colors. The plants in each were long dead. Allie resisted the urge to dump the contents just in case something was buried in all that potting soil.

Just because the FBI and cops had been here already didn't mean they wouldn't be coming back. No one would be happy with the news that Allie and Steve had been on the property having a look. Disturbing anything at all that would be easily noticed wouldn't be smart. They hadn't broken into anything—technically. But they were trespassing, and the foray into the garage was not exactly a legal move. Maybe not the barn either, no matter that it was fully open with only stall gates on one side.

She kind of liked that Steve wasn't afraid to stretch the boundaries. Another indication that he wasn't so perfect or so uptight.

The fact was she liked everything about him.

The distinct sound of an engine and then a car door slamming had them both lowering the pots they held.

The next sound they heard was someone shouting, "Hello." Female.

"Stay here." Steve walked around the end of the house toward the voice.

Allie wasn't inclined to follow orders at the moment, so she did the same, ensuring that he was well ahead of her and didn't notice.

A woman stood next to a white sedan. She held a shotgun braced against one shoulder, but the barrel was extended toward the ground. "This is private property," she stated, looking directly at Steve.

"Yes, ma'am." Steve came to a stop at the front corner of the house. His arms hung loosely at his sides. His hands visibly open. "My name is Steve Durham. I work for a private investigations firm, the Colby Agency, and I'm following up on Mr. Thomas Madison's death."

This was true. Mostly.

The woman leaned to one side and peered past him. "Is this your colleague?"

Allie came to stand beside him. "My name is Allie Foster. Mr. Madison was a friend of my family. I'm the one who hired Mr. Durham."

The woman was older than she had looked from a distance. Closer to seventy than sixty. She was trim and well dressed. Her light-colored hair was actually a very flattering shade of gray. And she appeared quite fearless.

"The FBI and the police have been here already," she said. "I can't imagine what you hope to find."

"We have a photo," Steve said, "if you wouldn't mind taking a look. It's a couple who associated with the Madisons, and we're attempting to identify them. We believe knowing who they are might be very helpful to our investigation."

She hitched her head for them to come to her, but she didn't put down the shotgun. "I'll have a look."

Steve went first. Allie stayed close behind him.

"Do you live nearby?" Allie wondered how this woman had known they were here.

"I live across the road. I saw you turn into the driveway. My husband and I always kept a watch on the place for Thomas. He traveled a lot with his work."

"You've been neighbors a long while," Steve suggested.

"We were here when he and Jane bought the place."

"You knew Jane well?" Allie hoped for more information on the other property.

"Well enough," the woman said without further explanation. She reached for the photo Steve held. She studied it for several seconds, then shook her head. "I don't recall ever seeing them." She handed the photo back to him. "Why do you want to find them? The photo is obviously quite old."

Allie took another photo from her purse and handed it to the woman. This one was of her parents. "What about this couple?"

The woman stared at the photo for a while, her face blank. Then she shook her head. "Never seen them before either." She passed the photo back to Allie. "Again, why are you trying to find people in old photographs?"

"We have reason to believe they may have information," Steve said. "It's important that we find them."

"I have no idea who they are. Now, obviously you've had your look around, so you need to go. I don't want to have to call the police and report the suspicious activity."

She kept her gaze on Steve. Wouldn't look at Allie. The idea that this woman way lying about not knowing the people pictured in those photos had a stranglehold on Allie.

"Alice and Jerry Foster," she said to the woman, ignoring her edict and waving the photo again. "They were my parents."

The woman blinked, then reluctantly dragged her gaze back to Allie. "I'm sorry for your loss, but I never saw them before."

"Did Thomas live here alone?" Steve asked, drawing them past the awkward moment.

"After his wife…Jane died," the nosy neighbor confirmed, "he almost never came home anymore."

Allie fired another question at her. "Did he sometimes stay at the McHenry property Jane's father gave them?"

The neighbor stared long and hard at Allie then. "I have no idea. I don't know anything about that property."

"Like this one," Steve said, "it looks abandoned. Overgrown. Didn't Thomas have someone to take care of the place?"

"There was a man who did the lawn mowing and things like that," she said, "but I haven't seen him in a while."

"Do you know his name?" Allie asked.

The woman shook her head. "I never spoke to him myself. Just saw his truck coming and going."

"When was the last time you saw him here?" Steve prodded.

She shrugged. "Maybe a month ago."

"There was no business info on his truck?" he asked. *Good question.*

"Nothing. Just a plain white truck pulling a black trailer with a riding lawnmower parked on it."

"I have a business card I'd like to give you." When she didn't argue, he reached for his wallet and removed one. "I hope you'll call me if you think of anything else that might be useful in our search for the truth."

She accepted the card but frowned at the question. "What truth?"

"The truth about who murdered Mr. Madison," Steve explained. "I'm sure you and your husband will feel safer when that person is identified and brought to justice."

Another series of slow blinks. "Yes, of course."

"Do you know what happened to Jane's mother?" Allie asked. "Her father passed away, but there was no mention of her mother."

The neighbor looked startled at the question. "Luellyn. Luellyn Talbert. She and her husband were estranged, but I don't think they ever officially divorced. She had nothing to do with the family."

"Is she still alive?" Allie wasn't sure yet why it mattered, but she needed to check off that box.

"As far as I know. The last time Thomas mentioned her, he said she was a resident at Our Home, an assisted-living facility on the other side of town. She's been there a good many years. Maybe seven or eight." She frowned. "Why would you want to know about Jane's mother?"

"We want to know about anyone who may have any insights into Madison's final weeks of life." Allie felt confident the woman understood this but wanted to ask just to get a response. "Or who might be able to identify the couple in the photograph I showed you."

The neighbor nodded, the vaguest of movements.

"Thank you, Mrs...?" Steve shook his head. "I'm sorry, I didn't catch your name."

"Gayle Fischer. My husband Frank and I live across the road."

"Thank you for speaking with us, Mrs. Fischer," Steve went on. "We're doing all we can to figure this out."

"Isn't that the job of the police or these FBI people

who've been coming around?" She looked suspect of Steve and Allie's motive for being on the property.

"I'm sure both the police and the FBI appreciate any help they can get."

She made a maybe-so face. "I'll talk to my husband. See if he has anything to pass along."

"Thank you," Steve said.

Fischer, still holding on to her shotgun, loaded back into her car. Before turning the vehicle around, she took a last, long look at Allie.

When the neighbor had driven away, Allie turned to Steve. "She knows me or my parents. Her reaction to their photo was different from her reaction to the mystery couple."

"I noticed."

"Should we drive over and talk to her husband?" Allie's pulse had started to race. These were people who may have known her parents. There were so many things she wanted to ask. So much she apparently needed to know.

"Not just now. We should go see Mrs. Talbert. If the FBI hasn't interviewed her yet, we have a far better chance at learning anything she may know."

Something else Allie liked about this man. He was really intuitive and could see the bigger picture.

He was exactly what she had needed to get through this.

Chapter Seven

Our Home
Route 14
Woodstock, 11:30 a.m.

The assisted-living facility looked nothing like Allie expected. As lovely as the wood and stone facade was, the landscaping along with the nature setting was what set it apart from the average property of its kind. The building sat back in a vast estate well off the road. Water features and living sculptures dominated the entrance. The cobblestone parking area gave the feel of a European resort.

Completely unexpected.

The lobby was a flurry of activity. With it being Sunday, there were lots of visitors. Again, the medicinal smell she'd expected was pleasantly absent.

Steve provided their names at the reception desk, and they were given visitor badges and directions to Mrs. Talbert's room. They had no idea about her physical or mental condition, but the fact that she was in assisted living versus a more comprehensive care facility offered hope that she might be able to answer questions.

When they reached her room, which was in the Caribbean wing, Steve pressed the doorbell. Since the resident they had come to see was ninety-three, they waited patiently for an answer rather than tapping the doorbell again after only a few moments.

Extra patience, Allie reminded herself, was sometimes necessary to reach a goal.

Steve checked his cell. Allie glanced around the corridor, appreciating the wall of windows opposite the long line of doors. Lots of sunshine and more of that purposefully manicured landscaping for the residents.

The shuffling sound on the other side of the door drew Allie's attention back there and suggested the lady had arrived at last. A rattling sound and then the click of a lock preceded the opening of the door. Allie drew in a deep breath and braced for whatever she might learn next.

Luellyn Talbert was not tall like her daughter, though part of the reason might be age. Her hair was white and woven into a loose bun. But it was her vibrant green eyes that reminded Allie of Jane Talbert Madison. Their eyes were exactly the same.

"Mrs. Talbert," Steve said with a charming smile, "it's very nice to meet you." He offered his hand. "I'm Steve Durham, and this is my friend, Allie Foster."

He'd changed his opening to something less official this time. Good strategy.

Luellyn placed her thin hand in his and gave it a shake. "Nice to meet you as well." She looked to Allie. Her gaze narrowed. "You look so familiar. Do I know you, dear?"

Hope budded in Allie's chest. "I believe you knew my mother, Alice Foster."

Mrs. Talbert's mouth opened in surprise. "Why, yes. Alice was Jane's friend. You look exactly like her."

"Thank you." She liked when people told her this.

"May we come in and visit with you?" Steve asked.

"I don't see why not." She turned and shuffled deeper into her room. "Come along and find a seat."

Steve waited for Allie to go first. The room was far more like the main living area of a small apartment. There was a tiny kitchen and dining nook as well as a generously sized living space. A small hall to the far left led to additional doors, likely the more private spaces, while the window-filled wall directly across the main living space looked out over the large well-appointed courtyard that separated the various resident wings. Allie doubted that all the little apartments had such a view. French doors provided access to that area.

Luellyn settled into what was obviously her preferred chair. Allie chose the twin chair. The two were separated by a table. Steve made himself comfortable on the sofa.

"If you've come to ask me about Thomas," the elderly woman said, "you've come to the wrong place. Thomas and I didn't get along. He didn't like me, and the feeling was mutual." She lifted one frail shoulder in a shrug. "Perhaps in the beginning we were fine. It's just hard to remember any good times since they were so very long ago."

"Actually—" Allie reached into her purse "—I was hoping you could tell me who these people are." She first passed along the photo of all three couples. "My parents and the Madisons I recognize, of course. It's the other couple I don't know."

Luellyn took her eyeglasses from the table next to her and propped them into place. After a time, she nodded, her attention fixed on the photograph. "This was taken at the house my husband gave Jane as a wedding present." She looked to Allie. "Jane held the most wonderful social gatherings there—the home was certainly well suited for such things. The floor plan was perfect for having a big family too. We all fell in love with the possibilities it offered. But they didn't live there very long. Not after what happened."

Allie and Steve exchanged a look.

"Would you share with us what happened?" Steve asked.

Mrs. Talbert blinked. She looked to Allie as if she had asked the question or maybe because she felt more comfortable addressing her since her mother had been Jane's friend. "Little Tommy died there."

"Tommy?" Allie held her breath. She'd found no mention of a Tommy in any of her research. Since Steve hadn't mentioned anyone by that name, he likely hadn't either.

"My grandson. Jane's only child." Mrs. Talbert smiled sadly. "He was only three years old. Such a precious, sweet little child. He was the spitting image of his father, other than his eyes. He had my daughter's vibrant green eyes. Jane and Thomas were so proud of him. In those days, Thomas would have died happy for no other reason than the blessing of that child." She looked away a moment. "But he didn't die. Our sweet Tommy did."

Suddenly the numerous framed photos around the room of a little boy came into vivid focus. Photos Allie had skimmed minutes ago without really registering. The child had big green eyes like his mother and thick black hair like his father. Now, Allie also noticed a young Jane and Thomas in one of the photos. Allie had been so focused on the woman, Luellyn, she'd paid scarcely any attention to the rest.

Allie waited for Mrs. Talbert to go on, while part of her already regretted having asked the question.

"It was the swimming pool. He sneaked out. Made his way to the pool...fell in and..." She exhaled a weary breath. "Jane tried to save him, but it was too late. As if that misery was not enough to bear, she had just found out she was pregnant with their second child, but the trauma caused a miscarriage. Jane was never the same afterward. Nothing I could do. God knows I tried. Nothing her father or Thomas could do. A few months later, Thomas moved them to a different home and then everything changed. He became secretive. Jane said he was rarely home. Always at work. Her father and I had to have an appointment to see Jane. Thomas didn't want us just showing up. It was very strange."

"What a terrible time that must have been," Allie said, though the word *terrible* didn't even begin to describe how devastating it must have been.

Mrs. Talbert nodded, the move barely visible. "When I refused to go along with his rules, Thomas cast me out. Said I could no longer see Jane, and when I refused to obey his edict, he took out a restraining order. Claimed all sorts of lies about my behavior. It was a nightmare."

Allie couldn't even imagine.

"What about your husband?" Steve asked. "Did he receive the same treatment?"

"He did and…" She inhaled a deep breath as if to fortify herself. "…that was the end of us. He blamed me for the loss of our daughter, and maybe he was right."

Allie would never understand that sort of behavior toward a good parent, and what this woman was describing was a caring mother desperate to help her daughter. Allie would give most anything to have had her parents growing up, which raised another question. "Why didn't Jane stop him?"

The flash of hurt in the older woman's eyes shamed Allie. "I'm sorry. I shouldn't have asked."

Luellyn waved a hand. "No. It's all right. That was a long time ago, and although I will never stop feeling the loss, I have learned to live with it. What choice did I have?" She appeared to think a moment about what she wanted to say next. "But to answer your question, for a while Jane and I had secret rendezvous." A slight smile returned to her lips. "We talked and cried together. It was sad that we had to hide this from Thomas, but it was the only way it seemed. The year after…we, she and I, had a little birthday celebration for Tommy."

She fell silent for a moment, the memory obviously difficult. "The last time I saw her was right after that celebration. She told me not to worry anymore, that Thomas had come up with a plan that would make everything all right. I tried to question her about it, but she said she couldn't talk about the details." She drifted into silence again for a beat, then two. "I never saw her again after that day. I tried going to their house when Thomas was at work, but no one answered the door. I called, but the phone number was changed to an unlisted one."

"Was Jane also having secret meetings with her father?" Steve asked.

"She would never say, and my husband, of course, wouldn't tell me anything. But after she went into seclusion, he came to see me and said he was worried about whatever Thomas was doing, so I'm thinking that perhaps he found a way to see her at least once more. Then, the next thing I knew, he'd had a heart attack and was gone."

"You suffered such losses during that time," Allie offered. "It must have been difficult for you."

"No one knows what it's like to lose a living child unless they've experienced it."

"Do you believe Thomas was somehow working all

that time to turn your daughter against you and her father? Perhaps it finally kicked in." Steve glanced at Allie as he asked this.

"The way I feel about Thomas Madison," Mrs. Talbert said with a sharp point to her tone, "I would love to say yes, but I believe there was some other reason. I think he was doing something to keep Jane happy and that he felt we wouldn't understand. I know he loved my daughter. But he eventually isolated her completely." She gestured to Allie. "Your mother was Jane's best friend. Not long after Jane shut me out completely, your parents were shut out as well. Alice came to talk to me about how sad it made her. She too mentioned being concerned that Thomas was…" She pinched her lips together as if to think a moment. "The term she used was 'out of control.' She promised to keep me posted about Jane, but less than a month later, she and Jerry had that horrible, horrible accident."

The idea that Thomas Madison may have had something to do with the accident caused an uncomfortable twinge to creep up Allie's spine.

When the silence dragged on a bit too long, Allie said, "Thank God for my grandparents. They took very good care of me."

She wanted to ask what efforts Mrs. Talbert had made for the next twenty years to try and reach her daughter, but it felt wrong to keep picking at that painful wound.

"You never said—" Allie nodded to the photograph Luellyn still held "—if you recognized the third couple."

"Aw, yes." Mrs. Talbert nodded, attempted a smile, then adjusted her glasses and focused on the photo once more. "Hmm. They do look vaguely familiar." She cocked her head, first one way and then the other. "Wait, I know. They were at Jane's Christmas party the same year this photo was taken." She looked to Allie. "A couple of years before your parents had their accident, I believe. Before my grandson died."

"Do you recall their names?"

Luellyn pursed her lips. "She was Lucille, and I believe her husband was Dennis." She shook her head. "But for the life of me I can't recall the last name. The only reason I remember her first name is the red hair. I thought of Lucille Ball when she was introduced to me. You can't really see her eyes in this photo, but she had the same bright blue eyes too."

Allie had thought the same thing when she first saw the photo. She'd certainly watched plenty of old Lucy episodes with her grandmother.

"Were they close with Jane and Thomas the way Allie's parents were?" Steve asked.

"They were new in town when I met them," Luellyn said. "I think the husband had just been hired by Ledwell."

"Do you recall if Lucille came to Jane's funeral?" Allie wasn't sure if the question would be uncomfortable for Luellyn, but it would certainly clarify whether the mystery couple had still been around as recently as three years ago. And it allowed her to ask if Luellyn had been at the funeral without actually asking. Surely Thomas Madison wouldn't have kept her from her own daughter's funeral.

"She was not. All the friends Jane made during her marriage were noticeably absent. It was a very small gathering. Not becoming of my precious daughter, I'll certainly say that. She would have invited everyone."

"Thomas must have spoken to you at some point during the service." Allie hoped this was the case. The idea of him ignoring her would only add to the horror that had been their shared history.

"He allowed me to sit in the front pew with him. He even hugged me when the service ended, but he said virtually nothing to me. He was anxious to get away, it seemed. Perhaps he had someone new already."

Painful. It happened that way sometimes. But there was nothing in the research Allie had done to suggest he'd had someone in his life even just before his death, three years after his wife's.

"Do you remember," Allie ventured, "Jane mentioning anything regarding my parents and the work at Ledwell? Or maybe some other problem with them?"

"Jane adored your mother," Luellyn said without hesitation. "The two did everything together. Tommy was just a year younger than you."

Allie hadn't considered that she and this Tommy were likely close in age. Maybe he was the reason she remembered the house with the pavilion and pool. Maybe they had played there together.

How sad it was that their families had been riddled with tragedy.

"I was there once when you and your mother visited. You and Tommy were going round and round outside, the sun trickling over your big smiles. It was such a nice day."

Allie felt her chest constrict. "Did my mother seem happy?" She put her fingers to her lips. She hadn't meant to ask the question. What difference did it make really? And yet, even after all these years, it was…still important to Allie. She felt confident her grandmother would have told her if her mother hadn't been happy, but having an objective observation would be useful.

Luellyn smiled at Allie. "How could she not be? She had a beautiful daughter. Her husband was the kindest man you would ever meet. Even Thomas often said that

Jerry was far too kind for his own good. But to answer your question, yes, your mother seemed very happy. As did you. If there were any sort of problems, she gave no indication whatsoever."

Allie was profoundly relieved. "Thank you."

Luellyn's face fell as if she'd just remembered something that pained her. "I remember Thomas making some statement…later." She shrugged. "No wait, I'm wrong. This was perhaps a year after that day when you and Tommy were playing. Maybe days after the accident that took your parents' lives. Yes, that's right, just before what would have been Tommy's fourth birthday. Christmas was only a few weeks away."

"My fifth birthday was in the January after the accident," Allie said, hoping to help prompt her memory. "I don't even remember Thanksgiving since the accident had just happened. But I do remember that it was the worst Christmas and birthday of my life."

"Thanksgiving." Luellyn held up a finger as if to emphasize the point. "Yes. Jane and I got together that last time. This was when she mentioned Thomas having a plan. She also said something like Thomas thought Jerry had grown too much of a conscience. I didn't understand what she meant and said as much. But she ignored the comment and moved on. Her brain worked that way after Tommy's death. Skipped around and sometimes obsessed over seemingly unimportant things."

"Seems an odd statement to make." Steve pointed out exactly what Allie was thinking.

"It does." Luellyn nodded. "I have no idea what he meant, but I heard through the grapevine that Ledwell was having growing pains. Serious growing pains. With the nature of the work they did, back in those days, one can only imagine the sorts of things you had to be willing to overlook."

She had Allie's curiosity cued up now. "You mean like ethical challenges?"

Those appeared to be the biggest stumbling blocks today in the warp-speed research and development of AI. Many wanted to take a step back, to slow down the forward momentum until better ground rules could be established. Some wanted it stopped altogether.

"I suppose so," Luellyn agreed. "Without a conscience for our guide, what might we humans be capable of under certain circumstances?"

A bell chimed somewhere in the apartment.

"That's my cue," Luellyn said. "We have a special lunch on Sundays for anyone who no longer has family to visit—or just for anyone who wishes to attend." She stood. "I hope you'll forgive me, but I never miss our special lunches."

Steve and Allie stood as well. "Of course," he said. "We appreciate the time you've shared with us already."

"It was so very nice to meet the two of you." She looked from Steve to Allie. "I hope you find the answers you seek and that you'll share anything you find about my Jane with me."

"You have my word, Mrs. Talbert," Steve assured her.

Allie and Steve walked to the main restaurant with Luellyn and watched as she joined her friends. Allie admired that, despite all the sadness in her life, the woman had managed to find a way to go on.

"I sure hope I'm partying and socializing when I'm ninety-three," Steve said.

"She certainly sets a high bar," Allie agreed.

Allie suddenly wondered why she had allowed so much time to pass without jumpstarting her life beyond work.

Fear, she decided. Fear of the unknown. Fear of the uncertainty. Keeping her routine was far easier than putting herself out there and wondering what would work and what wouldn't.

She furtively watched Steve as they made their way back to his SUV. Somehow this man had her thinking a whole lot more about what she should be doing for herself. Thus, the sudden interest in the future.

How ironic. After all this time of hiding and pretending not to notice the world going on without her, she unexpectedly realized she was missing so much.

Just in time to be framed for murder.

Steve braked at the end of the long drive before turning onto the highway. He shot her a sideways glance. "You worried about what Madison said about your father?"

Allie pushed the other concern away and nodded. "The timing is tough to ignore." She bit her lip. "Do you think my father was against something Ledwell was doing? Maybe strongly enough to make himself a target? The same as the others involved with the SILO project?"

"If the crash was no accident," Steve began as he pulled out onto the highway, "then there had to be an impetus—something that motivated the step. When you consider the work Ledwell was doing—is still doing—it makes a great deal of sense that there would be issues from time to time. Those issues couldn't be allowed to become a real problem, if you know what I mean. No backing down. Not when you were racing against competitors to achieve something so big—something no one else has."

"Like the first robot to look human," she offered. "To act human?" The various companies involved would insist those sorts of things were not the primary goal and had only recently become actual priorities. But what if that was a lie? In Allie's opinion, based on her limited knowledge, it probably was.

"Something like that, yes. At this point, I think it's safe to assume that if your parents' car crash was not an accident then it had something to do with the work at Ledwell—with SILO. That can only mean the company was doing something not acceptable for the time. Whether it was illegal or not, it may have been something your father wasn't willing to turn a blind eye to. And it was likely something the company wanted to keep secret."

"We need to find Lucille and Dennis." Allie needed someone who could tell them what had been going on at Ledwell twenty-eight years ago and why her father had to be silenced.

Was that also what had gotten Thomas Madison murdered? Had the burden of all those secrets suddenly grown too much for his conscience after all these years?

Chapter Eight

Steve would be the first to say that his family had never been the country club type, no matter what their address said about them. Martha, his mother, appreciated a nice home in a nice neighborhood that came with a good school district—no question about that. Quentin, his father, had gladly worked extra hard to see that his wife had the dream house she so wanted as they started their family.

The tri-level brick was far larger than they needed now that they were nearing retirement age, but they both loved the neighborhood so much neither would budge on downsizing. His mom insisted they were waiting on a smaller home in the same neighborhood to become available. Steve didn't see that happening anytime soon. It was that sort of neighborhood: people came and they put down permanent roots.

In the end, the decision to stay put turned out to be the right one when his older by two years sister, Amanda, ended up getting divorced and moving into the lower level with her two kids.

His mom could not be happier. The kids were in serious heaven because Nana and Papa rarely said no to any request.

For their special guest this evening, Steve's father had set up a buffet on the kitchen island. Everyone grabbed a plate, took a stroll around the island and filled it as they went. Then it was on to the dining room, where wine, water and lemonade for the boys waited.

When Steve had been a kid, both sets of grandparents were still alive, and his parents had believed in having a table large enough for the whole family to be together, thus the table for twelve.

Amanda and her kids sat on one side, Steve and Allie on the other with his parents at the ends. A family gathering was a nice change of pace. He hoped the camaraderie would help Allie relax a little after the intense forty-eight hours she'd endured. Either way, the food smelled great, and Steve felt confident Allie was as hungry as he was. He was glad for once his sister and her kids appeared focused on eating rather than arguing about who got to pick the after-dinner movie. With boys, one eight and one ten, getting through a meal without a battle was sometimes difficult, especially in the summer when there was no homework or time at school to have worn them out.

"Your mother and I were friends when we were kids," Quentin said to Allie.

She smiled. "Be careful, Mr. Durham, or I'll be asking you questions about her all night."

"Call me Quentin, please. As for questions, ask anything you'd like."

Allie nodded. "Quentin."

Steve cut into his steak, grateful that Allie appeared comfortable with his family. Family was important to him. He couldn't imagine being totally alone. That had to be difficult for her sometimes. As sure of that as he was, he hadn't missed how strong and seemingly resilient she was. He liked that about her.

Frankly, he liked a lot of things about her.

"Well," his mother spoke up, "I can tell you that Alice was a very nice woman who never met a stranger. When Quentin and I first married, I was a stranger to the neighborhood. I knew no one. Your mother went out of her way to be kind to me. Your grandmother too. Another lovely lady. And you should call me Martha." She flashed that signature smile of hers—the one that said everything was okay as long as you were here with her.

Steve was fairly certain he lacked any measure of objectivity, but his mother's smile was the kind that really could heal those wounds that couldn't be seen.

"Martha," Allie said. "Thank you. Do you recall much about my parents during the time just before the accident?"

Steve had known that question would be coming. "We spoke with someone," he explained before one or the other of his parents could respond, "who suggested there might have been issues with Allie's father and his work at Ledwell."

Quentin made a harrumphing sound. "Anyone involved with Ledwell generally had issues, particularly during that timeframe."

"How so?" Allie lowered her fork rather than taking the bite of salad there. She leaned slightly forward...intent on whatever words he planned to convey.

Quentin shared a glance with Martha. This look was also something Steve knew well. Did they say what was on their minds, or did they let it go? That brief, silent exchange was the pause they used to measure the worth of one decision over the other. The couple had been together so long they had this ability to communicate without words.

Steve couldn't help wondering if it was even possible to develop that kind of relationship these days. How amazing it must be to have that level of closeness.

"I don't mean to spoil this lovely dinner," Allie said when no one spoke, her cheeks flushing. "It's just important. Really important. At least to me."

"Of course it is." Martha reached out and gave Allie's hand a kind pat.

"There were rumors," Quentin said finally. "Rumors of bad things happening at Ledwell. The sort of things you might see in a science-fiction movie."

"Or a horror film," Martha put in. She shook her head. "There were protests outside the facility. People were spreading all sorts of frightening stories. It really was a scary time. That year—when your parents' accident happened—was particularly tumultuous. A number of employees had freak accidents—at home, not at work. One woman suffered a lethal electrical shock from her coffeemaker. Another man had an accident while fishing. They say he fell out of his boat and wasn't able to climb back in—yet he was a seasoned fisherman who always used a boat."

"And others," Quentin pointed out. "Obviously we can't say how your father felt about any of this or where he stood with the company. We can only say how concerned many in the community were about the company in general."

"It was an uncertain time," Martha agreed. "Ledwell employees and their families felt isolated—your mother told me this. They were looked upon as being culpable because of their employment. Alice said she couldn't go to the market without feeling as though everyone was staring at her with suspicion. Judging her for the company's perceived wrongs. It was a truly difficult period."

"Did you speak at length with her," Allie probed, "about her concerns? Did she say anything that may have led you to believe she was afraid?"

Martha stared at her plate for a moment. Steve hadn't considered how difficult this might be for his parents, his mother in particular. He was aware his parents had known Allie's parents…but maybe there was more they'd never said out loud before.

"The last time I spoke with her—" Martha lifted her gaze to Allie's "—Alice mentioned that she was very worried about her husband. She wouldn't say why, but I could tell she was, as you say, afraid."

"After the accident," Quentin picked up from there, "no one would talk about it. No one. Those of us not involved with Ledwell had no idea there was anything to talk about other than the tragedy of it and all the rumors buzzing around. Even twenty odd years later, we still don't for that matter. But when Steve told us you had concerns, Martha and I started to think back. There was something wrong about the whole situation related to that accident and the others that happened, but there's not a single comment, rumor, certainly not a headline I can put my finger on to explain the feeling. It was just a sudden series of blunt traumas that left a gaping hole in the community, and then it was as if it never happened. As if none of it ever occurred. In time, people stopped talking about it."

The way Allie's eyes shone now, Steve worried she was on the verge of tears.

"Did the two of you," Steve asked his father, "have

a chance to talk about the Madison child and what happened to him?"

Bringing up yet another tragic accident at the dinner table felt necessarily improper under the circumstances. Steve couldn't get past the fact that after leaving Mrs. Talbert, they'd found nothing online about the child's death. No obit. No headline. Not one mention. It was beyond strange. It was almost as if any record of the child and his death had been scrubbed from the internet. If Steve wasn't fully aware that it was possible to do exactly that, he would think the notion was a little on the unreasonable side.

But it was possible. It had been done more times than the average person realized. There were services available for the right price to make just about anything go away.

"We weren't really acquainted with the Madisons," Steve's father said. "We knew Alice and Jerry primarily because she and I grew up in the same school district. Our parents were friends. But Alice did talk to Martha a few days after it happened." He turned to his wife. "I remember you were quite upset about the conversation."

Martha nodded. "Alice told me about it. She and I were both flabbergasted that there was nothing in the paper after...what happened. Nothing at all. We discussed the idea that perhaps the Madisons had managed to keep it quiet to avoid all the painful drama. But I don't think Alice believed that. I know I didn't. I firmly believed that it was Ledwell's doing. It felt like they wanted to avoid any and all bad press no matter the circumstances. I didn't see her again for months." She frowned. "Maybe closer to a year. I remember it was only a few weeks before their accident. She seemed distracted and worried. *Unsettled.* I wish I had tried harder to find out what was going on."

Allie smiled, her lips trembling with the effort. "You couldn't have known. No one could have."

"Looking back, Allie," Quentin said, "I believe there was more to your parents' accident, and I am equally certain there was something the Madisons wanted to keep hidden about their own tragedy. The old saying hindsight is twenty-twenty is sadly true. We can see so much now that we didn't then. In part because we didn't realize we needed to look. Basically, we ended up chalking it all up to gossip and fear of the unknown. I mean, let's face it, even now the AI stuff is a little unsettling."

Martha nodded. "All that aside, there was something odd about some of the things that went on with Ledwell back then. Looking at each piece or incident individually—as we did when it was happening—it didn't feel so pressing, so overwhelming. But when you consider it all as a whole, it's entirely overwhelming."

"There's no question in my mind," Quentin went on, "that those same sorts of things are still happening. They're just better at hiding their secret activity these days. It's funny. With social media, the average person's whole life is out there for all to see. But those with the power can hide just about anything."

Steve knew all too well how true that statement was.

"I can't help wondering," Allie said, "if what happened back then is the reason Mr. Madison was…" She looked toward the kids. "Why he went away so mysteriously."

Steve noted that his sister was scrolling on her phone with one hand and lifting her fork with the other. As a single parent of two kids, she rarely got a moment to herself to do as she pleased. She took her moments where she could find them. He stifled a grin at the boys, who stared wide eyed at Allie, mouths slightly open.

"Don't worry," Amanda said as she glanced up at Steve, "they're really into mysteries right now. The scarier the better."

The boys, Clint and Carson, immediately launched into tales of their favorite true-crime episodes.

By the time dinner was over, Steve wondered if his sister was raising future investigators or serial killers.

While everyone else drank more wine and had cake, the future crime fighters retired to the den downstairs to catch up on whatever was streaming. Amanda insisted on cleaning up, and Steve and his father pitched in. His mom had family photo albums to show off to Allie.

When the cleanup was nearly done, his dad hitched his head toward the door. "Go on. Make sure your mom is not boring her to death."

Steve tossed the dry towel onto the counter. "You know Mom is never boring."

"You haven't lived with her as an adult," Amanda challenged from the refrigerator, where she was storing leftovers.

Steve laughed. "You talked me into it. I'll go check on them."

He found his mom and Allie on the sofa in the living room. The fact that they were laughing suggested there was no boredom with which to be concerned.

Allie held up a handful of photos. "Your mom gave me most of the photos she had that included my parents. One even has me in it."

Steve sat down beside her. "I didn't realize there were so many," he said to his mother.

"Neither did I. Oh." Martha raised a hand as if to rally their attention. "I think the mystery couple is Lucille and Dennis Reger or Regers. I'm not sure about the last name.

I ran into Lucille, the redhead, in the market. She was with Alice. She seemed very nice."

"That could really help." He smiled. "Thanks, Mom."

"I could ask around," she offered. "I still have a good many friends from back then. A few who even still work for Ledwell. Someone else might recall some relevant fact about the couple."

An alarm triggered in Steve. "As much as we appreciate the offer, I'd feel more comfortable if you waited a bit on any actions like that. We don't want to stir up any undue attention to what Allie and I are doing. We've already hit a number of roadblocks."

Her mouth formed an O, and she pressed her hand to her chest. "Oh my. I never considered this was more of an undercover investigation. You're right." She pinched her thumb and forefinger together and slid it across her closed lips. "I won't say a word to anyone."

"Thank you so much for the thought," Allie spoke up. "You've already been so helpful. Really. I cannot tell you how much it means to me to hear these details about my parents. My grandparents found it difficult to talk about that time, and I never wanted to press."

Martha smiled sadly. "I understand. I assure you, Allie, if we think of anything at all that might help, we'll call Steve and let him know."

Steve was surprised at just how quickly his mom and Allie had bonded. He was also surprised at how very much he'd missed family gatherings like this one. He had to make more of an effort to be here for these times. He watched his mother's vibrant expression as she spoke. No one was promised tomorrow. Something else he should be keeping in mind—especially when involved with a case like Allie's.

AN HOUR LATER, there was a round of hugs at the door in another Durham family tradition. Nobody left the house without a big hug and an *I love you*. Amanda hugged him harder than usual. While her cheek was pressed to his, she whispered, "She's a keeper. Don't let this one slip away, bro."

He smiled as he drew away. "I'll keep that in mind, sis."

She punched his shoulder. "Good. Be smarter than me."

As a kid, he would have tossed back that he already was, but as an adult he recognized how intelligent his big sister was and what a tough lesson she had learned about trust. Cheating spouses sucked.

Outside, the night had grown sultry. The June temps were record-breaking this year.

"Your family," Allie said as she settled into the passenger seat, "is really amazing. I love your mom."

"I think she's very fond of you as well." He closed Allie's door and walked around to slide behind the steering wheel. "I'm glad we were able to get together."

"I didn't realize how much I missed family dinners." She stared out the window as she said this.

"I had the same thought." The difference was, he still had that option. He wanted to say more, but he wasn't sure any words he drummed up would fill that void.

Instead, he drove through the darkness, his mind rushing forward to find a way to put the information they had gathered into perspective. He really enjoyed his work, but this was the first time it felt personal. Others had told him how difficult it was when a case crossed that line. Now he understood. It was a physical pain.

Allie relaxed deeper into her seat. "Thank you."

He glanced at her, grateful for the reprieve from his thoughts. "For?"

"For coming to my rescue." She turned to him as he slowed for a red light. "I know that sounds a little dramatic, but you could have said no. You could have put me off on another investigator."

"No way. This is what you do for friends."

"Well, again, thank you for remembering me and being my friend."

He almost told her how easy she made the effort, but he decided maybe that might be a little more forward than she would find comfortable.

"Home sweet home," she said as he pulled into her driveway.

He wondered if she actually saw it as home sweet home or home lonely home. The thought of her here alone so much of the time bothered him. A lot.

ALLIE WONDERED WHAT Steve was thinking as they climbed out of his SUV and walked toward her porch. He and his family had been so kind to her tonight. And more helpful than she'd anticipated.

The photos Martha had given her were priceless.

Steve unlocked the door and insisted on going in first. She locked it once more while he wandered through the first floor. Flipping a couple of switches, she turned off some of the exterior lights. She liked leaving them on for when she was out and would be returning home in the dark. But once she was here, she toned it down.

Until now, she hadn't really understood why her grandparents were so fixated on security. She so wished they had shared their concerns with her. On one level, she understood why they hadn't. They had wanted to protect her, and, honestly, she would likely have started looking into all these odd circumstances if they had. She supposed she should be glad they hadn't told her.

Putting the worries aside for now, she needed to find her phone charger. With all the calls and research she'd been doing, she had almost drained the battery.

If she remembered correctly, she'd left it in the bag from the store. Upstairs. In her room. Or maybe in her office. She headed that way, turning on the hall light as she reached the top of the stairs. In her bedroom, she grabbed the bag. "And there it is." She snagged the charger and headed back out of her room.

She'd almost made it to the stairs when she stalled. Her gaze had stumbled over something. She backed up a couple of steps. The door to her parents' bedroom was open. Hadn't she closed it? She usually left it closed. It was just a habit of hers. Same one her grandmother had. Leave a room, flip off the lights and close the door.

Moving in a sort of slow motion, she turned and took the two steps to the door. Her fingers slid over the wall next to the frame, turning on the light.

The room looked as if a small tornado had gone through it. She blinked twice, told herself she wasn't seeing clearly. Still the same. Her parents' room had been ransacked. Clothes and other personal items littered the floor. Drawers had been dragged out of their slots and left upside down on the floor. The closet looked as if someone had tossed a hand grenade inside.

Someone has been in the house.

She turned all the way around in the room. Maybe they still were.

But the door had been locked.

"Steve!" She backed out of the room as she shouted.

She looked right then left along the hall to ensure no one was coming out of another room.

The intruder could still be here.

"Steve!"

He was bounding up the stairs before his name stopped echoing in the air.

He looked from her to the open door and back. "What happened?"

"Someone's been here."

He crossed to the door and had a look inside. "Downstairs is clear. Let's have a closer look up here."

They walked from room to room, checked the usual places. Under beds, in closets, behind doors. There was no one hiding anywhere they looked.

"They're gone now," Allie acknowledged, "but someone was definitely here."

"No question. We can call the police and report the intrusion if you'd like."

She shook her head. "No. If we do, we'll just be alerting the FBI, and they'll likely show up again. At the moment, I just want to know how he or she got in the house."

"Should be easy enough to determine," Steve suggested. "Let's check the doors and windows more closely."

They returned to the first floor. The front door had still been locked when they arrived. It was doubtful anyone had entered the house from there in light of the three deadbolts, but Steve had a look anyway. No indication the locks had been tampered with.

"No scratches," he confirmed, "or other marks to indicate the locks were tampered with."

Moving on to the kitchen, they found the back door shut but unlocked. There was no deadbolt like on the front. Allie watched as Steve knelt and examined the lock.

"Oh yeah. Someone used a flat tip screwdriver or something like that to jimmy the lock. You need a new one installed on this door." He stood. "You need a dead-bolt as well. Makes their work more difficult. We can call someone tomorrow."

"Okay." She chewed at her lip. "I guess my grandparents never thought about it either. Seems strange in retrospect."

All this time, she'd felt so secure with her triple deadbolts on the front door. She should have had this door secured properly ages ago.

"You never had any reason to worry about it."

She nodded. Sounded better than just not thinking at all. "I suppose we can rule out the FBI. They've already been here. And they had a warrant, so breaking and entering wasn't necessary."

Steve chuckled. "No. This, I'm guessing, is either someone looking for something the FBI missed or someone who wants you to be afraid." He settled his gaze on hers. "Either way, we need to secure this door until we can get a new, proper lock."

"I have something I think we can use for that." She rounded up the longest screws she could find and the battery-operated drill driver she'd bought herself when she added shelves to her office.

"That will definitely work as long as you don't mind my marring the wood." Steve accepted the items.

"Mar away. I can repair that with a little wood filler and paint."

"As you wish." He prepared to secure the door.

"I think I'll clean up the mess upstairs and call it a night."

He frowned. "It's been a strange day. You handling all this okay?"

"Sure." She backed toward the door. "Thanks again for everything. Really. You've done so much."

He smiled, making her heart react. "No problem. Goodnight."

"G'night."

What she didn't tell him was that she was totally exhausted with all of it. She had realized she didn't know very much about her parents and the final year of their lives. But now she was certain she had no idea what really happened to them either. What little she did know from that time didn't feel like the truth anymore. But she was certain her grandparents would never have lied to her.

They couldn't have known. She refused to even entertain the idea.

Allie wasn't sure what she actually knew at this point. But she intended to find out.

Upstairs, she started with the closet. Rehanging clothes and tidying shoes and scarves. Her mother's two favorite handbags went back on their hooks. Every single item made Allie miss these people she'd scarcely known so much more. She missed her grandparents too.

It wasn't easy being alone. Funny, she hadn't really noticed so much until now.

This time with Steve and tonight's dinner with his family had been a stark reminder of what she was missing.

By the time her parents' belongings were put away, she was dragging. Steve paused at the door. Evidently he'd finished up downstairs. At one point, she'd felt certain she heard him talking. He'd likely had calls to make.

"Need any help?"

"It's done." She surveyed the room. She'd put the

framed photographs back where they belonged as well as the little trinkets her mother had cherished. Sadly, she only knew these things because her grandmother had told her.

"Did you notice anything missing?"

She shook her head. "Nothing. Whatever the intruder was looking for, it obviously wasn't here."

As she walked toward the door, she noticed something on the floor just under the edge of the bed. She leaned down and picked it up. It was another photo of the mystery couple. What in the world was it doing on the floor? She turned it over, and their names were written there.

Lucille and Dennis Reger.

Mrs. Talbert and Steve's mother had been right.

Allie studied the photograph. "I don't think I've ever seen this one." She passed it to Steve. "My grandmother was very meticulous with photos. She kept them all in albums or frames. None were ever loose like this."

As Steve examined the photograph, a thought occurred to Allie. "Maybe," she suggested, "the intruder didn't break in to take anything. Maybe to leave something."

"A clue he thought you might need."

Allie nodded slowly, her attention fixed on the couple in the photograph. "Maybe he thinks we need a little help."

"Or he's playing with us," Steve countered.

The kind of playing, Allie realized, that got people killed.

Chapter Nine

Monday, June 9
Chicago
Colby Agency, 8:00 a.m.

The elevator doors opened, and Allie stepped into the lobby of the Colby Agency.

This was exactly what she had expected based on all she'd read about the venerable Victoria Colby-Camp. The agency—the woman, really—was legendary. Whether you were in Chicago or Paris, those in the know recognized the Colby name.

The lobby was large and decorated in a sophisticated yet comfortable style. A glass desk that actually looked like a work of art stood in front of an enormous glass wall that showed off the breathtaking view of the city beyond it. Also behind the desk was a woman, who Allie decided must be a receptionist.

"Good morning, Ms. Foster." The woman, who was around Allie's age, smiled then looked to the man right behind her. "Mr. Durham, Victoria and Jamie are waiting for you."

"Thank you, Madeline."

Steve pressed a hand to the small of Allie's back and

gently guided her toward a long, wide corridor. Still gawking in an attempt to take it all in, she wondered how different these offices were from the original ones. According to her research on the Colby Agency, the original offices had been blown up by a longtime enemy. The family had withstood far more than their share of personal attacks and tragedy. But they were survivors with a truly incredible history.

Allie could not believe she was here. She only wished she didn't feel so underdressed. The black slacks were the closest thing to dressy she owned. The white button-down with the big collar was from forever ago. She'd spotted it online and had to have it. She'd worn it one other time besides today. The biggest change to her usual look was that she'd left her hair down.

She never did that.

She glanced at the man next to her. It was mostly because of him. He looked great. It was impossible not to feel lacking in style around him. His navy slacks and the lighter blue button-down looked amazing just because he was wearing them.

Good grief, she was besotted with the man. Which was only going to make it harder to say goodbye when this was over.

Dismissing the thoughts, she focused on this place and how lucky she was to be here. The agency hired only the very best and had a reputation for being the most discreet in the industry. She was so grateful to have this team on her side. She was reasonably certain she had told Steve this countless times already.

She sent him a sideways look. "This place is amazing."

He smiled. "It is. More than you know."

No doubt, she mused.

The desk in Victoria's private lobby was empty.

"Rhea, Victoria's personal assistant, is off today," he explained as he walked straight through to Victoria's door. He opened it and waited for Allie to go in first.

Always the gentleman. As old-fashioned as it sounded, she liked that too.

Holding her breath, Allie stepped into the head of the agency's private domain.

Victoria met them in the middle of the room. Allie had seen images of her online, but she wasn't fully prepared for just how awe-inspiring it was to be in the woman's presence. There was a sense of sophistication and wisdom that made Allie want to curtsy as if standing before a queen.

She definitely wouldn't say that out loud.

"Allie." Victoria extended her hand. "It's a pleasure to meet you. I've heard so much about you already."

Allie glanced at Steve as she took the other woman's hand. "The pleasure is mine, ma'am." She bit back all the new gushing compliments that came immediately to mind.

"Please, call me Victoria." She gestured to a young woman seated at the small conference table on the far side of the office. "This is my granddaughter, Jamie."

Jamie extended her hand across the table as Allie approached. "It's such a pleasure to meet you, Allie."

"The pleasure is all mine, I assure you." Allie couldn't help smiling as she shook the other woman's hand. She wore her blond hair down around her shoulders, and her blue eyes literally sparkled when she smiled. The gray sheath she wore looked as if she'd just stepped off a fashion show runway.

"Let's sit," Victoria urged, taking her seat at the head of the table. "The others will be with us soon. I'm aware you have another appointment, so we'll make this quick."

With those FBI agents. Allie wished she could forget about that meeting, but unfortunately it was impossible.

They all settled into upholstered chairs around the table just as three other members of the Colby team entered the office.

Steve made the introductions. "This is Nicole Reed Michaels and Simon Ruhl—he worked at the Bureau in a former life. He may be able to provide some insight into their agenda in your case."

"A very long time ago," Simon pointed out.

Allie smiled at the two. "Thank you for all you're doing to sort this mess."

"And this," Steve said, gesturing to the final arrival taking a seat, "is Jackson Brennan. He is a former bounty hunter and very, very good at tracking the missing and solving cold cases."

"Thank you," Allie said. "I am truly lost in all this."

Jackson gave her a nod. The man was tall, young. Midthirties maybe. If she were a bad guy and this man was tracking her, she would be very afraid.

"You needn't worry," Victoria assured Allie, drawing her attention to the head of the table. "We will get to the bottom of things as quickly as possible."

"We've tracked down the mystery couple," Jamie said. "They moved from Woodstock to Yuma, Arizona, twenty-six years ago. They declined to be interviewed by phone or in person. We have a local contact who showed up unannounced and made an attempt, but Mrs. Reger shut it down."

Allie's heart sank a little. She was really hoping the couple would be willing to answer questions. The husband having been employed at Ledwell and the two being friends with her parents had given Allie such hope they would know something helpful for moving forward.

"We've also looked," Nicole spoke next, "into the death of the Madison child, Tommy. There was no autopsy conducted—at least not in the state of Illinois—and the single document related to the child's death that we did discover indicated his remains had been cremated. This document was from a funeral home in Woodstock. The Wembley." She looked to Allie then. "But the part I found strange was that there was nothing else. No further indication that he died or that he was even born. No birth certificate. No medical records that we've been able to locate. We've been searching every available database for the past twenty-four hours, and there is simply nothing."

"Are you suggesting," Steve spoke up, "that the child was perhaps not the Madisons' biological child? Maybe there was an adoption they kept secret for whatever reason."

"That's possible, of course," Nicole agreed. "But what I've found is that, for all intents and purposes, this child did not exist. Not on paper."

"How is that possible? There were photos of him," Allie spoke up, "at the grandmother's house. Basically everyone we've spoken with who knew the family recalled the child."

"Private adoption," Steve suggested. "Illegal adoption."

"We ran his description," Jackson said, "through more databases to see if a child matching that description was reported missing during the target timeframe. Not a single name popped up. Then we searched for infants and toddlers in that category. The few we found who fit the search criteria were part of cases that were all solved favorably."

"It's possible," Nicole explained, "this is why there

was no coverage of his death. If the child had been stolen, the last thing the Madisons would have wanted to do was have photos of him in the news."

Allie's heart had started to pound at this new scenario. "What I'm getting from this is that my parents may have somehow figured out the child was stolen, and they were killed to prevent them telling others what they had discovered."

"It's certainly a theory that merits consideration," Victoria agreed. "There are documented cases of personnel having bizarre accidents and people protesting the work being done at Ledwell, which we, as you know, believe to be the primary scenario related to the possibility of how the accident happened. I fear we'll have to dig much deeper to find anything one way or the other. The person or persons behind all this have been very careful in covering their tracks."

"But there were no investigations," Allie said. "At least, none that were conducted officially. How can we prove these allegations or suspicions if we can't get anyone to talk?"

"None we've found so far," Victoria reminded her. "But, in my experience, if you poke at a bear you'll get a reaction. Maybe not the first time, but he won't ignore you for long."

Allie smiled. She really liked this lady and the way she thought.

"I've reviewed the accident report from the night your parents died," Simon spoke up. "Mechanical failure is the only cause listed—which you already knew. The deputy who was first on the scene and who investigated the accident is retired now." To Steve, he said, "I've forwarded his contact information to you. Unfortunately, the mechanic mentioned as having conducted the actual examination of the vehicle has since died."

"The reporter," Nicole said, "Rivero, may be an important link in this chain of information. If you can get him to talk—" this she directed to Steve "—he could provide useful details."

Steve nodded. "We'll get him to talk."

Allie was still reeling with all she'd heard when it was time to go. As she and Steve rode the elevator down to the main lobby, she tried to remember if she'd thanked everyone. They were all working so hard—even using their weekends—to help her find the truth.

Without the truth…she could end up being charged with a murder she didn't commit.

Federal Bureau of Investigations
Roosevelt Road, 10:00 a.m.

ALLIE FELT COLD. Her nerves were fluttering. Palms sweating.

She wanted to scream that she had no idea what any of this was about, but that was no longer true. She understood that it was about the past, and somehow her parents were involved. Allie also got that there were things—secret things—that were being kept from her to cover up for other secret things…none of which were good.

Steve had said that powerful people sometimes went to great lengths to conceal their tracks. Allie understood this. She might be a bit of a recluse, but she didn't live under a rock. Still, his telling her was valid. Most people—even those aware that things like this happened—didn't really recognize just how deep, just how bad these cover-ups could be. Most people were like her, she supposed.

She walked through life believing others were good until something happened to change her mind.

Evidently that wasn't true in some cases.

Driving up to the FBI's complex felt like arriving at a prison. A three-building complex of concrete, steel and glass stationed on twelve acres with mazes for parking lots and other things—little box-shaped metal things—she couldn't identify.

Inside was a whole other story. The lobby was certainly not one found in any prison with its endless glass and marble panels for walls all showcased by granite flooring and meticulously placed plants and stylish seating areas. The ceiling soared two stories with all that glass allowing sunlight to fill the space. They might have been in a luxury resort hotel on a tropical island somewhere.

Special Agent Fraser met them in that grand lobby.

"Thank you for coming." He looked to Allie as he spoke.

Like she had a choice.

"We'll be going up a few floors, where we'll catch up with Agent Potter in a private conference room."

"Lead the way," Steve said, cutting straight to the chase. No smile. No handshake. Not even a hello.

Allie reminded herself to breathe as they rode the elevator upward. Fraser said nothing. Steve said nothing. Allie was ready to erupt with tension. But then Steve glanced at her, smiled, and she felt better. Calmer.

Funny how that worked.

The elevator stopped, and they prepared to exit. Fraser started forward then abruptly paused and indicated that Allie should precede him. She did so and waited for the two to join her in the corridor. Other staff members hurried along to meetings, speaking quietly to colleagues going in the same direction or to someone via a cell phone.

They all appeared focused on their own agenda, intent on some destination, and not a single one paid the slightest attention to her and the two men accompanying her.

The conference room was small but private. Agent Potter was already seated at the oval table. A large binder sat in front of her. Next to the binder was a medium-sized box, flaps closed, concealing whatever was inside.

The fluttering nerves were back.

Potter gestured to the remaining chairs around the table. "Find a seat and we'll get started."

Steve pulled out a chair for her, and Allie lowered into it. She focused on slowing her respiration. Reminded herself that she had a secret weapon—the Colby Agency. And Steve. She watched as he settled into his chair. She relaxed. He had her back.

"I'd like to start this meeting," Potter said, "by passing along that we have confirmed the video provided by hospital security was edited."

Allie barely resisted the urge to do a fist pump and squeal.

"That's not to say," Fraser added with a look directly at Allie, "that we're convinced you had nothing to do with or have no knowledge of the events leading to Thomas Madison's death. But we are aware of this aspect and wanted to let you know."

Her glee vanished. "I'm sorry. I don't see how you can still believe I'm involved. I didn't even know the man."

"I'm assuming," Steve said, "you're looking into who had access to surveillance systems at the hospital."

"Of course," Fraser confirmed.

Potter opened her binder and turned it toward Allie

and Steve. "In your parents' room—in the home where you live—we discovered these."

The first plastic sheet protector held a blank page with two photos mounted on it. One photo was of Thomas Madison coming out of a local market. The next was of a vehicle—presumably his—turning into his driveway. Based on his age in the one at the market, the photos were recent.

"I've never seen these photos before." Allie shook her head. What the heck was this? "You couldn't have found these photos in the house. They don't belong to me, and no one else lives there."

"These photos are recent," Fraser pointed out. "Just days before he was hospitalized and murdered. And they were found in your home."

Potter turned the page. More photos of a similar nature. Allie shook her head again. "I can't help you with this." She turned her palms up and gestured to the binder. "I don't know anything about these."

Clearly they were photos taken by someone following Madison around, but that person wasn't her. Until Friday night, she'd had no clue who he was or that he even existed, for that matter.

"But these photos were also in your home," Potter repeated. "You surely saw them. They weren't hidden in some out-of-the-way place. They were in the drawer next to the bed."

Allie tried to think when she'd been in that room last, much less prowled around in the drawers. The door stayed closed, and she went in there once in a great while to dust and vacuum, but she never searched or even touched anything beyond moving a framed photo to dust or something like that.

"I'm telling you," she insisted, "I have not seen these photos before."

Her mind went immediately to the photo she'd found in her parents' room today. She'd never seen that one before either. Maybe the person who'd been in her house yesterday had been in there before. She decided not to mention as much. If Steve wanted the agents to know, he would tell them the story.

Potter flipped over to another page. "What about these?"

The photos were of her parents and the Madisons. With the mystery couple captured on the edge of one of three snapshots. Allie wondered how much the FBI knew about the couple. The Colby Agency had located the couple, but they refused to talk. The two were a dead end so far.

"I recognize my parents and the Madisons—only because of what has happened since Friday night."

"This is the Regers." Potter tapped the image of the mystery couple. "They were assets of the Bureau working at Ledwell at the time your father was employed there."

Allie and Steve shared a look. No wonder the couple refused to speak with anyone from the Colby Agency.

Steve turned up his hands. "Ms. Foster has already explained that she has no knowledge of these photos or how they came to be in her home. I suggest we move on."

Potter turned to the next page. This one showed a series of photos of a vehicle Allie didn't recognize parked in front of her house. The photos appeared to have been taken at different times, maybe on different days. She couldn't be certain, but the vehicle was parked at slightly different locations. The shade from a nearby tree hit the vehicle at barely perceptible variances in each photo.

She looked to Potter. "Someone has been watching my house?"

Potter nodded. "Thomas Madison."

Allie shook her head. This made no sense. "He never

came to the door. If that's him, I had no idea he was there." She looked Potter straight in the eyes. "Why would he be watching my house?"

"We have no idea," Fraser admitted. "We hoped you might be able to tell us."

Allie held up a hand. "This man was part of an investigation you were conducting prior to his death." She looked from one to the other. "You mentioned this in our first meeting. Why didn't you tell me he had been watching my house? And how did you get these photos?"

"We're asking the questions here, Ms. Foster," Potter pointed out.

"We can't help you solve your case. We have no reason to believe any part of it is connected to Ms. Foster, and she had no prior knowledge of the details you've revealed." Steve gestured to the binder. "My guess is someone is playing you. Trying to derail your investigation. For all we know, Thomas Madison was losing his grip on reality before he died. Whatever the case, I believe it's pretty clear that Ms. Foster is not involved. You're far too focused on a woman who has no idea who Thomas Madison was rather than the identity and motive of the person who wanted to take his life."

Potter and Fraser exchanged a look.

"There's one more thing," Fraser said.

Allie couldn't wait to hear this one.

"Thomas Madison," he went on, "was murdered with an injection of phenobarbital into his IV fluids."

A large enough dosage was one way to put someone down, certainly. It didn't take a medical professional to understand how that sort of thing worked.

"You're a nurse," Potter pointed out. "You would know the drug to use and how to inject it."

"So would anyone else who bothered to google it," Allie countered. Now she was just angry. This was enough.

"Funny that you mention googling," Potter said. "We found several searches on your laptop about the best ways to cause sudden death."

Allie's jaw dropped. That was impossible. "I didn't do any such searches," she argued. Her skin flushed, and a combination of fear and outrage roared through her.

Steve turned to her. "We're done here, I think."

Allie was more than happy to hear that.

"You're going to have to do better than this," he warned the agents, "if you plan to keep dragging my client through these emotional minefields."

He stood. Allie did the same.

Potter pushed the box toward them. "Your laptop and other devices."

Steve took the box. "Good day, agents."

As they moved toward the door, Fraser spoke up. "Be careful where you step in this minefield, Ms. Foster."

Maybe she was a fool, but Allie turned back to hear what he had to say.

"We still haven't figured out all the players, much less who the true bad guys are."

She gave a dry laugh. "Maybe because you're looking in the wrong place."

Allie walked out. She had nothing else to say. But she couldn't help wondering if the agents were the bad guys because they damned sure seemed intent on framing her.

The one thing she was certain of in all this was her innocence.

She just hoped Steve and the Colby Agency could help her prove it.

Chapter Ten

Wonder Lake
Rivero Residence
Lake Shore Drive, Noon

Steve knocked on the door after two attempts to rally the resident with the doorbell.

Rivero knew they were here, and they knew he was in there. He had the cameras, and his vintage SUV was parked near the door like before. It was backed up to the house as if the owner wanted to ensure a swift and unencumbered getaway.

"He's not going to answer." Allie's shoulders sagged.

The meeting at the Colby Agency had buoyed her hopes, and then Potter and Fraser had sunk them with their ridiculous accusations.

"He will answer as long as he's still breathing," Steve argued. He fisted his hand and rapped again, hard enough to rattle the door on its hinges. "Because we're not leaving—" he stared directly at the camera "—until he does."

"If you keep pounding on my door," Rivero said, his voice sounding scratchy over the speaker, "I'm calling the police."

Steve pulled out his cell phone and stared up at the camera. "I'll do you one better. I'll call FBI agents Potter and Fraser and tell them you're ready to talk about all the secrets you uncovered at Ledwell. Particularly those about the child, Tommy, and his parents' strange behavior after his alleged death."

Thankfully, Allie concealed the surprise she might be feeling at his statement. His goal was not to make her think he knew something he hadn't shared with her. His intent was to get the guy to come to the door. It was a strategy he hoped to hell would work. They badly needed a break—sooner rather than later.

The release of locks clicked in the silence that followed.

Steve resisted the urge to grin. *Gotcha.*

The door opened and Rivero stood there, a couple of feet back from the actual opening, as if he feared catching something or being yanked out of the house by the collar of his hoodie. For such a former hotshot, his look had gone to hell. Sweatpants and a hoodie. Unshaven and his gray peppered hair badly in need of combing.

He exhaled a big breath. "Come in. Let's get this over with."

Steve flashed Allie a knowing look. She walked in, and he followed.

Rivero locked the door behind them. Like Allie, he had multiple deadbolts.

Then he led them deeper into the house, to a large main living area that looked out over the lake through a wall of glass. Not a bad view.

The former star reporter gestured to the sofa and then took a seat in what appeared to be his preferred chair. The leather recliner showed the wear of its preference, whereas the matching sofa looked new.

"What do you want to know?" He looked from Steve to Allie. "I can't promise I'll answer every question you ask, but I'll give you what I can."

When Allie started to speak, Rivero held up both hands stop-sign fashion. "Be aware that I'm only doing this because Fraser and Potter are closing in on a court order that I may not be able to ignore. I'd love to get a step ahead of them."

Good to know the two agents were rattling his cage as well.

"What do you know about the accident that killed my parents?" Allie started with the issue closest to her heart.

Steve wasn't surprised that was her first question. This thing that had begun haunting her less than seventy-two hours ago had reopened that old wound, relentlessly tearing at it.

Rivero considered her question for a time before responding. To make something up? To figure out the best lie? Who knew.

Now that Steve was this close, he noted that beneath the I-don't-care attire and lack of grooming the man didn't look so different from the way he had than two decades ago. He'd allowed his hair to gray, but he still looked fairly lean for an older man. Judging by the equipment on the other end of the room, he stayed fit. Weights and a stair climber as well as the latest in bike machines. The eyeglasses were new. Or maybe he'd worn contacts back when his face was all over the news channels. If not for the downgrade in his appearance, he might still look the part.

"Your father," he began, "was young, not so highly educated and a bit naïve when he started with Ledwell."

Allie shifted in her seat. No doubt feeling the sting of his blunt words about her father's education level.

"You mean he wasn't Ivy League educated like the scientists at Ledwell," Steve corrected.

"Of course that's what I mean. The place was full of pompous geniuses." He looked to Allie then. "Don't get me wrong, your father was a brilliant man. He had the kind of brilliance an expensive university couldn't give. That's why Ledwell wanted him."

She visibly relaxed. Steve wanted to keep her that way. This was tough enough without added nonsense.

"There were rumors of trouble," Allie said. "I found a few news reports, headlines in papers online but nothing deep or revealing. Nothing that ever prompted people, much less the authorities, to sit up and take notice."

"That's because Ledwell owned everyone back then. The press, the powers that be, they all said what Ledwell wanted them to say. When I tried to find a damned outlet that would publish my story or let me tell it in an interview, no one would touch me. I ended up blackballed." He looked away a moment, stared out that enormous glass wall. "I had to get away. I disappeared for a while. Wrote the book." He shrugged. "Who knows, maybe one day it will be published."

"What was *your* story?" Allie prodded, shifting gears like a reporter herself.

Steve kept quiet. Let her do the asking. Reporters liked when a story was personal. This was as personal as it got for Allie. The connection would be stronger with her.

He looked from Allie to Steve and back. "I need to know that you aren't wearing a wire of any sort."

Frankly, Steve was surprised he hadn't attempted to strip search them when they first entered his home. Maybe age had slowed him in that respect as well.

Rivero got up and picked up a device from the table

next to his chair. "If you're carrying anything electronic, this will pick it up."

Steve stood and removed his cell phone from his pocket and placed it on the coffee table. He stepped away from the sofa, held up both arms. "That's all I have."

Rivero moved the device over his body from the tips of his fingers to the ends of his toes. Careful not to miss an inch. When he was finished, he nodded and turned toward Allie.

She opened her purse and took out her cell then placed it on the coffee table next to Steve's. Rivero checked her purse then scanned her body as he had Steve's. When the man nodded, Allie sat down. She tucked her cell back into her purse.

Steve settled onto the sofa once more.

"I heard rumors that Ledwell was going beyond the established limits in their AI research and development. No surprise really. They were all doing it to some degree, but something about the way Ledwell operated gave me pause. Made me want to find the dirt. Eventually I found myself a whistle-blower. A janitor, Harvey Culver, who worked the evening shift." He fell silent for a moment. "This was a year or so before your father's death. This janitor was keeping an eye out for me. Reporting back what he saw. I bought him a camera he could easily conceal to snap pics of whatever he thought might be of interest to me."

Again, he paused and stared out that massive window wall for a time. "This went on for a while. It wasn't like he could bring me something after every shift. It was only on those rare occasions when no one noticed him around and allowed an opening for him to see something or hear something. The wait was difficult but necessary."

"Did you eventually learn the details that would give you the story you were after?"

He looked annoyed at Allie's question, but it was a perfectly logical one.

"You don't look for something that will give you the story you're after, Ms. Foster. The story draws you to it, and you look for the evidence that will confirm what the story is telling you. A true reporter doesn't create a story. He reveals the truth of the story that seduces him—lures him in."

Steve got it, but he didn't see the need to be so dramatic. "Which was?" he prompted.

"That Ledwell was way ahead of everyone else. Twenty-nine years ago, they already had robots that looked and behaved so much like a human it was nearly impossible to decipher between them."

Allie looked to Steve. He wasn't completely surprised, but she appeared to be.

"It was a race," Steve suggested. "What made this so newsworthy?"

"They were using human…" He hesitated. "Human parts in their development. Granted these were humans who had left their bodies to Ledwell for R&D, or so that was the claim. But their work was outside the parameters of what was considered ethical at the time. The laws…" He shrugged. "Were reasonably straightforward in those days. Not like now, where there's so much ambiguity. To tell the truth, I can only imagine what they're doing now." He looked directly at Steve then. "Whatever you imagine, multiply that times about a thousand. We should all be scared."

"How did my father play into your investigation? Was it because he was part of SILO?"

Like Steve, Allie recognized that was where this was going. She had hoped this man could shed some light on at least some of the unknowns.

Rivero stared at her for a long moment before responding. "We don't say SILO out loud. We don't text about it. We don't talk about it period. It was the CIA's baby, and that will get you taken out quicker than a dose of cyanide."

"We'll take that as a yes," Steve fired back.

Rivero held up his hands. "To answer the first part of your question, when the janitor died suddenly—"

"How did he die?" Steve interrupted.

"An accident, what else?" Rivero shook his head and considered his inspiring view yet again. "The official conclusion was that his truck fell off the jack onto him while he was working under it."

Allie winced. Steve sent her a reassuring look.

"I watched your parents for weeks to find the right opportunity to connect with your father." He took another of those long pauses. "There was a carnival in Woodstock. Your parents took you. I followed them, and while your mother rode with you on the carousel, I approached. A crowd of fathers and grandfathers were gathered in a cluster to try getting photographs of their offspring aboard the wooden horses. I pretended to be one of them. I got as close to your father as possible and told him who I was. In those days, I always wore disguises when out in public. It was the only way for me to have a moment of peace."

"Comes with the territory," Steve pointed out. From the videos he'd watched of Rivero's heyday, he had loved every minute of it.

"Why my father?" Allie asked, the ache of the question in her voice. "Why not someone else?"

"Harvey had given me the names of those who knew

the most and who I might be able to trust. I certainly didn't want to approach anyone who would out me. Otherwise, I might have ended up under a car like poor Harvey."

"Or dead on the side of the road with your wife."

Allie's words hit their mark. Rivero grimaced.

"The truth was," Rivero went on, "Jerry was looking for a way out. He'd been contemplating just leaving town. Taking his family and disappearing. But your mother wouldn't hear of it." His gaze settled on Allie once more. "Your mother didn't want to leave her parents, and they refused to move."

Allie's expression warned that his words stabbed deep. Steve knew she had loved her grandparents. The idea that a single decision on their part caused this had to be immensely painful.

While she struggled for what to say next, Steve asked, "What about the Regers? Dennis and Lucille? Were you watching them as well?"

"The redhead." Rivero nodded. "Those two were a bit on the strange side. The husband, Dennis, was from Germany. He spoke with a heavy accent. He'd met Lucille in New York when he moved to the US. He'd decided to take a short vacation there before continuing on to Woodstock to join Ledwell. They had recruited him from a competing firm in Berlin."

Steve understood now. Lucille was likely the FBI connection. Apparently, the Bureau had been watching Ledwell even then.

"I'm sure your friends at the Bureau told you they were assets," Rivero said, echoing Steve's thought. "It was actually Lucille who was the agent. Dennis was the target she turned once he was in position at Ledwell."

"If the FBI had some idea what Ledwell was doing

all those years ago," Allie spoke up, "why did they allow them to continue with research and development that was not allowed at the time?"

Rivero laughed. "Well, Ms. Foster, if you haven't learned this yet, let me bring you up to speed. The government works in mysterious ways. They were willing to keep an eye on Ledwell in hopes of making sure the government benefited. Besides, the CIA gets what the CIA wants. The trouble was, Ledwell was aware. They were very careful about what they allowed to be disseminated to the government. They used Dennis Reger to pass along what they wanted the Bureau to know. This, of course, was the CIA's idea. The two agencies do not play well together. If Potter and Fraser tell you differently about any of this, it's only because they're ignorant of the actual facts or they're in denial. At this point, I'm stunned the feds even still fish around Ledwell. They're clearly getting what they want, or this would have ended years ago."

"Did you warn my father that what he was doing by helping you might be dangerous?"

Steve understood she felt her family had been betrayed by this man, and they likely had been. But he doubted that her father had not been aware of the risk, perhaps not to his family but certainly to himself.

"He was well aware," Rivero insisted. "We all were. He saw things that troubled him, and he couldn't live with the idea of keeping those secrets. When two of his colleagues on the team died under suspicious circumstances, he was ready to do something."

"Do you have proof of what he and the janitor saw happening?" Steve wasn't sure it was even relevant at this point, but there was no statute of limitations on murder.

"I had what I needed to do my story." Rivero didn't

actually answer the question. "I had photos and copies of documents."

"Had?" Steve nudged for clarification.

"My office was robbed. My home. My car. They found and destroyed everything." He tapped his temple. "Except what I have right here. They couldn't take that because I vanished before they got the opportunity."

Steve shared a look with Allie. This was the reason the much-touted story never surfaced. It was why he'd never gone to anyone who might be able to stop what was being done at Ledwell. Because he had no proof of what he believed—beyond what was in his head.

"Do you believe they killed my parents?"

"Of course they did. Just like they killed four other members of his team as well as Harvey and no doubt anyone else who got in their way."

"Do you have proof of any sort?" she demanded.

He shook his head. "Jerry was bringing me proof that night. He and your mother were taking you and leaving right after he met with me. Your grandparents had figured out something was very wrong and urged them to go. That night, he would give me what I needed, and then the three of you would disappear. But he never came. Hours later, I followed every route between his home and where we were to meet until I found the car in the ditch, almost hidden from view."

The pain that captured Allie's face then made Steve's chest tighten.

"There was nothing I could do for them. They were dead. But—" he took a big breath "—I searched the car, and whoever killed them had obviously already taken the files because I found nothing." He stood, walked to the fireplace and wiggled a stone free. He removed something from the space behind it and brought it to Allie. "This was clutched in your mother's hand." Then he plopped back into his chair as if he'd dealt his final hand and was waiting for her to top it or to fold.

The delicate silver chain wasn't large enough for a necklace. A bracelet, Steve decided. Tiny silver blocks hung on the thin line of silver.

"This was my baby bracelet." Allie's eyes filled with wonder. "My grandmother said my parents put it in the time capsule they made when I was born."

Rivero must have had the same thought as Steve because they both asked at the same time, "What time capsule?"

"The day I was brought home from the hospital," she explained, seemingly unaware of their tension, "my parents added this bracelet and both my and my mother's hospital bracelets to the time capsule they had prepared. They buried it in the backyard."

Rivero turned to Steve. "If they took this out of the time capsule because the mother wanted to take it with them when they left—" the man had to take a moment to get his emotions under control before he could go on "—maybe the only thing they planned to give me was the location of the time capsule." He stood, started to pace. "It makes total sense. That way they wouldn't be caught transporting the only evidence that existed outside the walls of Ledwell. Oh my God, all this time. Why didn't I think of that? The bracelet meant nothing to me." He turned to Allie, his entire being on alert. "We have to find that time capsule. *Now.*"

Foster Residence
Ridgeland Avenue, 2:30 p.m.

ALLIE WASN'T SURE they had fully convinced Mr. Rivero they would keep him apprised of what they discovered.

He'd called every twenty minutes for the past hour and a half. He wanted to come but hadn't been able to bring himself to leave the house. Allie had read about and watched movies and documentaries about people who couldn't leave their homes, but she'd never seen it firsthand.

"I'm sorry." She wiped the sweat from her forehead with the back of her hand. "I really thought it was in the butterfly garden." She remembered seeing photos her grandmother had taken of the big day. Allie looked around. "It was right here." She surveyed the various flowers and shrubs that attracted butterflies, all surrounded by a cute little picket fence.

"We should have a look at those photos if you know where they are."

"Good idea." One she should have thought of nearly two hours ago.

She hurried into the house and to the bookshelves where all those photo albums were stored. It took a minute, but she found the one that held the photos from that year—the year she was born. Her grandmother had been very careful to ensure all her albums matched and all were dated with a gold metallic marker. It was an obsession of hers, she'd said.

Allie flipped through the pages, found the right one and grinned. The butterfly garden had been a lot smaller then. She carefully removed the photo that provided the best overall shot of her father digging the hole.

She hurried back outside to where Steve waited, sleeves rolled up to his elbows and the shovel in hand. Like her, he'd started to sweat quickly in the afternoon sun.

"This is it."

He wiped his hand on his thigh and accepted the photo. After studying it at length, he turned around slowly, surveying the garden enclosed with that white picket fence. At least it had started out white. It had faded and chipped in places. Something else Allie needed to take care of.

He pointed to one of the lilac bushes. "I think it might be under part of that bush."

Allie bit her lip. The lilacs had been her grandmother's favorite. "Be really careful. I'd hate to kill the bush."

He pointed his shovel toward it. "There are times when sacrifices must be made."

She laughed, mostly because she was emotionally drained and physically spent. The small silver bracelet felt cool in her hand, but she couldn't bear to let go of it. Her mother had been holding it when she died. And this was for her parents. "Just do it."

It didn't take a lot of imagination to conjure up images of her parents rushing out here in the darkness of night to dig up the time capsule they had planted four years prior. She could see her father doing what he had to do once it was out of the ground, stuffing evidence inside while her mother picked through the mementos that had been hidden there. Allie could see her holding the delicate silver chain—the very one she now held. Tears burned her eyes, and she forced away the images.

Get this done, Al.

To his credit, Steve took his time and used extra care when digging around the base of the bush. At last the blade of the shovel slid into the ground, and there was a distinct metal-on-metal sound.

Steve smiled, crouched down and started to dig with his gloved hands.

Allie held her breath, afraid to hope but unable to stop herself.

The dirty object he withdrew didn't look like the one in the photos. A frown worried her brow. Wait…

He wiped the dirt away, and there it was…the stainless-steel cylinder-type canister she'd seen in the photos.

Maybe she would finally have the evidence she needed to uncover the truth.

Chapter Eleven

3:50 p.m.

After Steve had covered all the holes made to protect the lilac bush, they brought the canister inside. Despite her earlier insistence about the bush being her grandmother's favorite, Allie really hadn't wanted to take the time to cover the holes, but Steve pointed out that the agents could show up at any moment. It was best not to leave anything too obvious for them to find. They couldn't ask about something they didn't know.

And she and Steve weren't sharing this find with anyone—at least not until they had time to evaluate what they actually had.

Now, after waiting patiently for longer than she wanted, Allie's heart was about to burst from her chest. Steve struggled to get the canister open. Her father had closed it tightly, and it had been in the ground for more than three decades. A serious round of elbow grease and some extra time was required, but he finally loosened the top. Then, without so much as a peek inside, he handed it to Allie.

She nodded and gave the twist-off top a final turn. Holding her breath, she turned it up to pour the contents onto the table.

Nothing came out.

Allie shook it harder. Still nothing. Panic building, she looked inside. Oh, okay, there were papers stuffed inside.

The evidence Rivero had been looking for?

Allie unfurled the paper…not evidence. A newspaper from the day she was born. She set it aside and turned up the capsule once more. This time several items tumbled out. A baby rattle. She touched it, smoothed her fingertips over the pink flowers painted on it. Then there was a shoe, her first presumably. She tucked a finger inside, found nothing. A silver spoon. And photos. Several of Allie and her parents along with a couple of her with her grandparents.

Disappointment bled through her. "Looks like it's a bust."

"Maybe." Steve had opened the newspaper and was perusing the pages. He smiled. "Copy this down."

Anticipation zinged Allie again. She pulled out her cell, which promptly rang again with a call from Rivero. She tapped the decline button and opened her notes app. "Ready."

"L…o…o…k. Look," he murmured.

"Yep." Allie's finger was poised for the next letter.

"H…r…w…s…e…h…e…e…"

"Where or here…he or she," Allie said as she put the letters in order to spell out whatever words best fit.

"Here's more," Steve said. "R…i…b…u…d…e." He flipped through the pages. "That's all the circled letters I see."

Allie couldn't help grinning at the idea that her mother or her father had thought to send a message this way. "Where she…where he's… Does the *s* have an apostrophe with it?"

"Damn." Steve turned back to the necessary page. His gaze bumped into hers. "It does. The final word is *buried*. Where he's buried."

"The child?" Allie nerves were jumping now. "Where the little boy's remains are buried."

Steve skimmed the pages once more. "That has to be it." He folded the newspaper carefully and put it aside. "So where is Tommy Madison buried or were his ashes spread somewhere—assuming he actually was cremated?"

Her cell started to ring again. This time, she answered. "There was no evidence in the time capsule." She waited until Rivero finished spewing expletives. "Do you know the location of the little boy's final resting place?"

Rivero did not know where the child was buried, but he did know the name of the man who had worked at Wembley Funeral Services at the time of his death—a man who liked his Jack, as in Jack Daniel's, when he could afford it. Allie ended the call with another promise that she would keep him up to speed on their movements.

"He gave me a name and an address." Allie gathered the precious items from the time capsule and placed them back inside. "We should go there."

Steve grabbed his keys. Allie decided she wasn't leaving the time capsule here for someone to break in and steal. At this point, she didn't trust anything or anyone... except this man.

Griggs Residence
Shady Acres Mobile Home Park
Barrington Road, Wauconda, Illinois, 5:00 p.m.

ALLIE LEANED FORWARD as Steve drove slowly through the mobile home park. They had found a liquor store on the way and bought the gift they hoped would get the man talking. Mitchell Griggs, former funeral home attendant, lived in a rental about twenty-five miles from Woodstock.

Only he didn't use the name Griggs. He went by Mitch Butler, his mother's maiden name, according to Rivero. He'd left Wembley Funeral Services only a few weeks after Tommy Madison died. No one had heard from him for a while, then he'd shown up at another funeral home, this one in Chicago, but he'd used the Butler name. He'd been using it since.

There were many reasons why a person would want to disappear and to change his identity. Allie got it. Sometimes she thought about doing exactly that. But she only needed the answer to one question from Mitchell Griggs, aka Mitch Butler.

What really happened with the little boy?

Maybe two questions.

Why all the secrecy?

Steve parked. "You want me to do this one alone?" He glanced around. "This place looks a little sketchy."

"No way." She reached for the door and grabbed the bottle of Jack with her other hand. "I'm going with you."

They exited the SUV and climbed the steps to the small deck. The numerous shade trees made the hour seem later than it was. The place was low rent for sure, but it was all the dark corners and narrow alleys between the rows of homes with their overflowing trash cans that gave it that truly sketchy feel.

Allie had just raised her fist to knock on the door when it opened outward. She stepped back, bumping into Steve in the process.

The man, short, thin, sixtyish, eyed her up and down then glanced at Steve. He had the tiniest eyes. Beady eyes and thin hair that had once been black but was mostly gray now. "Whatever you're selling, I ain't buying. If you're from the police or any other law enforcement organization, come back with a warrant."

"None of the above." Allie extended the bottle like a peace offering. "I'm Allie Foster, and this is my friend, Steve Durham. We're here to ask you about a little boy who died twenty-eight years ago. Tommy Madison."

The man grabbed the bottle from her at the same instant his openly suspect expression closed like a slammed door. "I don't know what you're talking about. I never heard of any kid by that name."

"You worked at the Wembley Funeral Home," Steve countered, "where his body was prepared."

The other man shook his head. "You got the wrong guy." He started to close the door.

Allie stepped into its path, blocking it with her shoulder. "We know you did, Mr. Griggs. We're not here to cause trouble. We just want to ask you a couple of questions."

His eyes narrowed to an even beadier size. "Now why in the world would I answer any of your questions?"

"My father was Jerry Foster. He worked for Ledwell back then. I think they killed him and my mother in a car accident. I just haven't been able to prove it."

He barked a laugh. "I really can't help you now. I want no part of that kind of crap."

This time, Steve reached above Allie's head and caught the door when Griggs would have tried to pull it past Allie. "Where was the child buried?"

Griggs blinked. "Who said he was buried?"

"The dead are usually buried," Steve argued.

Griggs heaved a put-upon breath. "I know I'll regret

this." He looked at the bottle he held. "The kid was cremated."

"Now that wasn't so difficult, was it? Look, you don't have to invite us in." Steve hitched his head toward Allie. "But you do need to answer her questions."

Allie bit her lips together to prevent smiling. She really liked this guy.

"You're certain you didn't hear anything about where he would be buried? If—" Allie amended "—he was going to be buried?"

Griggs leaned against the doorframe. "I was curious, so I hung around that evening. I heard the father say something about taking him home to bury him."

"But you're certain they cremated him," Allie pressed. "It's important, Mr. Griggs."

"I put him in the furnace myself," he said with a covert look side to side. "That was my job at the time—when there was a call for it. Cremation wasn't as popular then as it is now. Especially when it involved kids."

Allie could certainly understand why. It would be a difficult decision. "Why did you leave Wembley a few weeks later?"

He shrugged again. "I changed jobs a lot back then. Why not? They all paid the same. I could walk down the block and get another job doing something completely different, and I'd still get paid minimum wage."

Valid point.

"According to Wembley," Steve spoke up, "you were discovered in a compromising position with one of the female—"

"That was a lie." Griggs pointed his finger at him. "They made that crap up because they wanted to scare me. They knew what I'd seen, and they wanted to make sure I stayed quiet." He sneered. "Don't pretend to know me or understand what I've been through in my life. I know what I saw."

"What did you see, Mr. Griggs?" Allie asked. "I think it may have been related to what got my parents killed."

He studied Allie for a long moment before deciding to respond. "Why does it matter? Really? Finding the truth won't bring your folks back. It won't make you feel any better about them being dead. So what's the point? I mean, these dudes are too big to bring down. If that's your goal, that will never happen. Digging around in this will get you the same place it got your folks—dead."

"You leave that part up to me, Mr. Griggs," Steve pressed. "We won't use your name. We just need to know what you know about the little boy. Then we'll leave you alone."

"Fair enough." He shifted his attention back to Allie. "But don't make me regret trusting you. If some form of the po-po shows up here after you leave, I'm gonna—"

"They won't," Steve inserted, his words a little on the lethal side.

"The parents brought the kid in. They were both distraught, you know. Tore all to pieces, like you'd expect. They waited while I did what had to be done. But—" he cast another of those furtive looks first right then left "—before I took him back, the mother leaned down and kissed him. Not unusual." He shrugged. "But she whispered something to him. Not I love you or something you'd expect."

"What did she say?" Allie asked when his dramatic pause went on a beat too long.

"She said, 'Daddy will bring you back.' It freaked me out a little, I have to tell you."

A chill raced over Allie's skin. "Did you see or hear anything else?"

He nodded. "When I prepared him for the crematorium, I noticed something weird. Trust me, I've seen some weird stuff in my time—working with the dead, I mean. But this was really creepy considering that one of the parents would have had to do it."

"What exactly did you notice?" Steve prompted. "If you could be as precise as possible."

"His eyes were missing." He patted one eyelid. "You know, the whole eyeball."

Allie's heart stumbled then started to race. "You're certain?"

He nodded. "Oh yeah. I checked. I'm sorry, but that is just bizarre. Who takes their own kid's eyes? I mentioned it to the manager later, and he told me never to talk about it again. It was a matter of discretion. He said I'd be fired if I ever mentioned it to a soul. So I didn't ask anything else, but I did talk about it with a couple of guys at the pub. I was a little drunk. I guess it got back to the wrong person. The next thing I knew, I was being followed."

"You're sure someone was following you?" Steve countered.

Allie could understand why Steve would be skeptical. The guy gave off a less-than-reliable vibe. Still, what he'd said so far made her feel ill.

"Definitely. I've been the target of drug dealers, loan sharks, pissed-off broads, I know when I'm being followed. It didn't take me long to figure out who it was. Especially after that sleazebag reporter, Rivero, tracked me down. I knew it was Ledwell. Damn it. I knew it, and I got the hell out. I had heard what those bastards did to people who saw things and dared to talk."

For a moment, Allie couldn't find her voice. Of course the idea had been in the back of her mind that Ledwell had been taking care of anyone who might dare tell his secrets. Rivero had confirmed as much…but this was the sort of affirmation that made her worry about what she might find at the end of all this.

Didn't matter. She was on a mission to find the truth about her parents' accident and to prove she did not murder anyone. "Did you happen to overhear the Madisons mention what they planned to do with his ashes?" She really needed to know where he was interred.

You planning to dig him up?

Allie banished the voice. If that was what it took to find answers then…yes. Maybe.

Griggs drew in another of those big, exaggerated breaths. "The wife mentioned she wanted him with her roses. Whatever that means."

Allie's breath stalled in her lungs. She knew exactly what that meant.

Talbert/Madison Residence
Justen Road
McHenry, Illinois, 7:00 p.m.

THIS HAD BEEN Jane and Thomas Madison's home at the time of their son's death. Mrs. Talbert, Jane's mother, had explained as much. This was the place where they entertained their friends and probably business associates as well. It was the place where their son died. *This* was the place where Jane had grown her roses.

The backyard was shrouded in shadows now. They had very little daylight left, but they had to try.

Steve had brought the shovel from her house. He had

started to dig amid the overgrown rose bushes. Allie held a flashlight to aid their ability to see between the overrun shrubs. When he'd loosened most of the ground around the fountain and the rose bushes were out of the way, she got down on her knees and picked through the loosened clumps. They didn't have any gloves—they'd forgotten them—but she didn't care. She needed to find an urn or box. Something!

Steve knelt beside her and dug in as well. The more she plowed her fingers through the dirt and found nothing, the tighter desperation banded around her chest. There had to be something here. There just had to be. Tears burned in her eyes. This could not be another dead end.

But there was nothing. Not unless they had buried the child's remains far deeper.

"We can try again tomorrow," Steve promised as he dusted off his hands.

Allie dusted off her hands as best she could. "You're right. It's too dark…we're not prepared. Tomorrow will be better."

She was exhausted, and she was certain he was as well. It had been a very long day, and it wasn't as if they hadn't made some new discoveries.

Baby steps.

Like those of a little boy who was buried around here somewhere. Maybe with evidence that would prove Ledwell had reason to want her parents, a janitor and God knows who else dead.

On the way back to the SUV, she called Rivero and gave him the bad news. He didn't take it well. The man was such a jerk.

Back at his SUV, Steve loaded the shovel, and Allie watched the last of the light sink into the treetops. She

wished she could remember the times she had been here…
the things that happened… Had she played with that little
boy more than once? Had she overheard hushed conversations that might help her now?

"Hey." Steve came to her at the passenger-side door
and gave her a hug. "We'll get there." He drew back and
smiled down at her. "Don't worry."

"Thanks." She dredged up a smile. "I needed a hug."

"I thought you might. What do you say we go home
and crack open a bottle from your stash?"

"I say that sounds amazing."

As did a long hot bath and maybe a nice salad.

And some time just to be.

Thankfully, Steve had a package of wet wipes in his
SUV, and they were able to reasonably clean their hands.
Her whole body pulsated with something…an urgency
she couldn't label. Maybe what she needed was to feel
something more…a connection to another human—like
this man.

Don't get ahead of yourself, Al. This is work for him.

Besides, now wasn't the time. She needed to focus.

The drive back to her house felt as if it were taking forever. "We should just grab something at a drive-through,"
she suggested. There was nothing at home. She really did
have to do a better job of keeping her pantry and fridge
stocked. She was kind of pathetic at the job.

She thought of the baby bracelet. Why the hell had
Rivero kept it all this time? And why didn't he talk to
her the first time they went to his house? The whole idea
infuriated her now that she thought about it. Particularly
after he'd basically hung up on her when she told him
they hadn't found anything beneath the roses at the for-

mer Madison home yet. He'd been furious they had dared to leave rather than continue to dig. *Jerk*.

Like Griggs said, Rivero was mostly a sleazeball.

"We can do that. Just name your preference."

"I'm easy," she assured him. "Just pull in at the next place we pass."

Blue lights suddenly throbbed in the side mirror. Allie twisted around in her seat. A police cruiser, lights blaring, nosed up behind them and sounded off a quick burst of its siren.

"What the hell?" Allie turned to Steve. "Were you speeding?"

"I was not." Steve slowed and eased to the side of the highway. "I guess we'll find out what I was doing."

Allie could not remember the last time she had been pulled over by the police. But then she didn't do a lot of driving, so that wasn't making a point at all.

Steve powered his window down and placed his hands on the steering wheel.

The officer took his time getting out and then approaching their vehicle.

Allie just wanted to go home. She felt more tired than she had in her entire life.

A flashlight pierced the interior of the SUV. She squinted to block the blare.

"License and registration," the officer demanded.

Steve reached for his wallet, removed his driver's license and handed it to the officer. "Is it okay if I reach into the glovebox and get the registration?"

The officer studied his license and then shone the flashlight directly in Steve's face. "That won't be necessary, sir. I need you to step out of the vehicle."

Allie's pulse reacted. Was this normal procedure?

"I will step out of the vehicle when you tell me the reason you pulled me over and why you need me to get out."

"Sir, there's an APB out for your arrest, and I'm going to need you to come with me. You can call your attorney once we're at the station. But I would prefer that we not have any trouble here on the street."

Steve held up his hands. "I'm certain there's been a mistake, but I'm happy to cooperate. If you'll allow me, I'd like to make a call and confirm that the APB is actually for me. I believe I'm well within my rights to request confirmation."

"If you'll step out of the vehicle, sir," the officer repeated, "you can make the call from my patrol car."

"I'll make it now," Steve countered. "We'll go from there. I'm an attorney. I know my rights."

"I'll stand by." The officer didn't move or take his flashlight's beam off the two of them.

Steve picked up his cell from the console and made the call.

Allie's frustration and anger mounted with every second that passed. This was ridiculous. How the hell could there be an APB out on Steve?

"Thanks." Steve ended the call. "Looks like I'm taking a ride to the city jail."

"This is insane," Allie argued. "You haven't done anything."

"Don't worry," he assured her. "My team is on it. You can follow us there. This shouldn't take long to clear up, but I need you to follow us there and stay within view of the officer manning the lobby at the jail."

"You should go home, ma'am," the officer spoke up. "This may take some time." He opened the driver-side door.

"Follow us," Steve repeated. "I want you nearby."

"I will."

Allie watched in horror as Steve was handcuffed then escorted to the cruiser and placed in the backseat. What the hell was going on here?

She climbed across the console, settled behind the steering wheel and adjusted the seat. When the police cruiser pulled away from the curb, she did the same. She followed the vehicle through the dark streets. This was so wrong. She shivered. But what could she do? How did she prove it was a mistake?

Maybe she should call Rivero. He might have a contact with the police from back when he was such a big news star. There likely weren't very many people in this little town that he didn't know.

But that had been a long time ago.

Then again, the Ledwell group didn't just know people. They appeared to own people. How did you stop a machine like that?

Not alone, for sure.

Steve had called his people. The Colby Agency would know what to do. If anyone could stop them, it was the Colby Agency.

Chapter Twelve

Allie sat in the lobby, frustration roaring inside her. What the hell were these people doing? She glared across the room at the desk sergeant. She wanted to rant at the woman. But it wasn't her fault.

The molded plastic seats were incredibly uncomfortable. Allie shifted to another position. The tile floor and walls were basically the same color, a sort of off-white. The place reminded her of what she imagined a morgue would look like.

The officer who had pulled them over had taken Steve beyond those double doors that required being buzzed in to pass through. She was left to sit here and wait. Her mind kept whirling with the bits and pieces that had come out today. Not that any of it added up to a firm answer, but it was starting to come together toward one. Rivero kept sending her text messages asking what was happening. She'd given him the short version of events, and he'd only responded with Oh.

Yeah, she mused, *oh*. He hadn't mentioned knowing anyone who could help, so her decision not to call him had been the right one.

She got up and started to pace. She could not sit still a moment longer. The desk sergeant watched her for a moment then returned to whatever she was doing on the computer. Allie figured the people who sat behind that desk saw plenty during a shift. She wasn't about to give anyone a show. Her goal was to walk off some of the building agitation.

The walls suddenly felt as if they were closing in on Allie, and she couldn't breathe. She walked to the desk and fixed a smile on her lips. "I'm going out to the car for a while," she said to the woman beyond the glass. "I'll be back in a few minutes."

The woman nodded but said nothing. It wasn't her job to keep up with Allie or to provide information to Steve about her whereabouts. Why had she even walked over and said anything?

Whatever.

Allie crossed the sterile lobby and pushed through the exit door into the muggy night air. She drew in a deep breath and glanced around. The parking lot was quiet. A few other cars but no sign of people. She walked to Steve's SUV, unlocked it and climbed inside. She pressed the lock button immediately. She surveyed the parking lot again to make sure she was alone. Another hard shiver passed through her.

Maybe being outside wasn't smart, but she couldn't be in there anymore.

She needed to do something.

Her phone buzzed with another text from Rivero. She rolled her eyes and returned a message of Still waiting.

She tossed her phone onto the console and stared at the bracelet the man had kept all this time. She fingered the tiny silver blocks engraved with the letters of her name. Her mother had been holding this bracelet. Had she thought it would be a good-luck charm? Or just a way to cling to her love for Allie while they did what they had to do in hopes of escaping?

What had her father known that put them in such danger? What if the newspaper had been a ruse, and she and Steve had missed something in the time capsule? Her brain felt under pressure from all sides. She couldn't get a deep enough breath. Allie shook her head. She had to do something, or she was going to have a full-blown panic attack. Taking care, she placed the bracelet in the cupholder on the console, then she reached into the rear floorboard and grabbed the time capsule. She opened it up and removed the contents, placing each item on the passenger seat.

She flipped on the overhead lights and started with the newspaper. Maybe the circled letters were the ruse. After all, they were a little obvious. Even the message, now that she thought about it, was in-your-face recognizable. Her father was too smart for that. Allie smiled. If she had learned nothing else, she had discovered how very smart her father was and how loving her mother was.

Taking her time, she reviewed each headline, each ad for local shops and businesses. The classifieds received a thorough read. How many spies had used classifieds? Her father would have considered that as well.

Thankfully, the paper didn't consist of that many pages, so her work wasn't too terribly time consuming. Nothing jumped out at her. She moved on to the photos. She shuffled through them one at a time, taking in every detail of the image. Most of them were taken in the backyard at home. Nothing new or notable in any of those either. Then she picked up the shoe. She smiled. It was so tiny.

She wondered if she'd actually worn it at all since the time capsule was buried the day she was born. Maybe from the hospital. On the other hand, it had been dug up later when evidence was supposed to be added. But her parents wouldn't have had adding sentimental items on their minds at that time.

Nothing in or on the shoe. No writing. Nothing. The spoon was just a spoon. Stainless, not real silver. No brand engraved on the handle. Lastly, she reached for the rattle. It wasn't one of the fancy silver ones. Just plastic. Yellow with pink and blue flowers.

She looked it over carefully, gave it a good shake. The rattle didn't sound the way she'd expected. She frowned. More a plunk effect than a clatter. She traced the seam where the baby toy was put together, and her finger stopped then went back over the right side of the seam. There was a tiny piece missing on the little lip on the one side that closed over the other. In that area, the two sides felt as if they weren't pushed together all the way. She studied it more closely. The sides appeared to have been pulled apart and then shoved back together. Her gaze traveled down the length of the now vintage toy to the part she held in her palm. The stem or handle had been broken and maybe glued back together.

As if someone had broken the handle while prying apart the two sides of the round end that held whatever was supposed to make the rattling sound.

Allie hesitated for only a second, then she started to tug, using her fingernails, which were dirty from digging, to pry at the narrow little gap in the seam. She couldn't get it. Damn it. She needed a screwdriver or…maybe a key.

She dug in her purse until she found her house key. After placing the rattle on the console, she held it in place with the fingers of one hand and jabbed and pried at the seam with the key in her other hand.

It took a bit, and she cracked the bigger part of the rattle to get the job done, but it opened. Rather than small beads or something on that order to clatter around inside, there was a small, slim, silver object. She picked it up, her eyes communicating what she saw to her brain but her gray matter rejecting the idea.

Thumb drive…flash drive…whatever one chose to call it. It appeared to have a small cap. She tugged it free, and sure enough, there was the USB port plug.

"No way," she murmured.

Instinctively, she reached up and turned off the light, anticipation soaring through her.

Then she sat, unable to move or really think, for a moment.

This couldn't be…

Her parents had died twenty-eight years ago. About three years before flash drives were available on the market for everyday consumers…but they had existed. She knew this from some movie she had watched, and she'd been certain they'd made a mistake, but she googled it, and sure enough, the writers had been correct.

Still…she should check again. She looked at the name on the tiny little device.

Allie grabbed her phone and searched flash drives and the name. She remembered correctly. They did exist—this brand in particular—well before they were widely available on the market.

Okay. Her disbelief drained away. This could be loaded with evidence. From her father. About Ledwell and SILO.

What the heck was she thinking? Of course it was. It was in the time capsule that *they* had buried, and it was inside her baby rattle. What else would it be? Anticipation seared through her veins. Her right leg started to pop up and down.

She glanced at the police department building. There was no way to know how much longer Steve would be. Her house was like two miles from here. All she had to do was rush home, get her laptop and come right back. No biggie. Ten minutes tops.

Heart pounding, she hit the start button on the SUV and drove out of the parking lot. She drove slowly, maybe too slowly. So possibly the trip would take fifteen minutes. She couldn't remember the last time she'd driven anywhere, so slow was likely the best option. Even at her turtle-like speed, it took her a whole fourteen minutes to make the short trip.

She turned into her driveway. The house was so damned dark. If she'd had any idea they would be gone so long she would have left the outside lights on. She shuddered as she parked. She could do this.

She could.

Just because someone had killed her parents and several other Ledwell-associated people didn't mean she was in that same sort of danger.

The storage device clutched in her right hand seemed to grow warmer as if warning her to think again.

Don't be naïve, Al.

Before getting out, she sent a text to Rivero and told him that she may have found something and had come back to her house for her laptop. She left it at that. No need to give him any other specifics. Then she sent a text to Steve's phone. It had most likely been confiscated, but he needed to know where she was just in case he came out in the next ten minutes before she was back in the parking lot.

She surveyed the darkness outside the vehicle. She had lived in this house her entire life. Played in every corner of this yard. At one time, she had known all her neighbors. Granted, this was an old neighborhood, so the houses were farther apart than in newer communities, and there were trees—lots of trees. Lots of hiding places.

She banished the notion. She knew every tree. This was home. Not some wilderness she'd never explored.

Deep breath. She opened the door and climbed out. She touched the door handle and locked the SUV. Continually scanning the darkness for movement, she tucked her cell into one back pocket and the fob into the other. Clutching her house key and with the flash drive in her front pocket, she hurried to the door. She unlocked each of the deadbolts with the key. Every click making her look around to ensure no one had appeared out of the shadows. The back door was still an issue, but Steve had screwed it shut from the inside, so that wouldn't be easily used by an intruder. This door had been locked, so it wasn't likely anyone had gotten in again. She relaxed a little.

Of course, there were plenty of windows to be broken and climbed through.

She shook off the thought.

"Focus," she muttered.

The door opened into the little entry hall, and she flipped on a light switch. She breathed easier then. No one jumped out at her. No sound of running footsteps. It was all quiet. Since Steve had arrived, she'd been forgetting to set the security system, not that it would have alerted anyone, but it did make enough noise to probably deter a would-be intruder. She would be sure to set it when she left this time.

"Okay." She closed and locked the door, all three dead-bolts, then put the key in her front pocket. Moving quickly, she went from room to room, turning on lights, to ensure all was clear before heading upstairs.

Once in the second-story hallway, she checked the rooms up there too. When all appeared clear, she hurried to her office and reached for her laptop.

She froze, the laptop in her hand.

Why drive back to the station to have a look? Why not look right now? Assuming the contents weren't password blocked or somehow encrypted, she could see what she had in like ten seconds.

She really should get back.

But what if this was the information they had been looking for that would lead them to the truth?

Her need to know won the battle.

She slid into her chair and opened the laptop. It took a moment to get the flash drive into the proper port. Even more time was required for it to launch and load.

"Come on," she muttered, her nerves jumping.

Then it started.

Holding her breath, she watched as folders loaded onto the screen. None were labeled beyond the basic numbers 1, 2, et cetera.

She clicked on the first folder and, sluggishly, it opened. Dozens of documents populated the screen. She clicked on the first one, and it opened. The title on the page was Test Subject One. The accompanying image had her jaw dropping.

The detailed description of the head…the shoulders and

torso…arms…legs…was that of a man except it wasn't…
human.

But it looked human.

She read through the notes quickly. Daily reports…
monthly progress.

Heart pounding, she closed that one and opened the
next. Another of the same, only this one was a woman.

"Holy…"

Glass shattering downstairs made her jump.

Allie stilled. Listened.

There was a sound…

She strained to hear…too terrified to move. There was
a crackling noise.

What the hell?

More shattering glass.

She yanked the flash drive from the port and started
to shove it into her pocket but decided to put it in her bra.
Moving soundlessly, she eased to the door. No one in the
upstairs hall. She crept along toward the staircase, listening and watching.

What was that smell? Gasoline.

She paused at the top of the stairs.

The distinct sound of a whoosh filled the air.

Fear rammed into her chest.

Fire.

She had to get out of here. Couldn't go downstairs…
whoever had started the fire was down there somewhere…
maybe waiting outside the door.

Slowly, she backed away from the staircase. She could
go out a window.

But she was on the second floor.

Allie hesitated, then she smiled. Didn't matter. Her

grandparents had put in an emergency ladder. Her grandmother said Allie's father had insisted.

"Thank you, Daddy," she murmured as she rushed to
her grandparents' room. There were three windows…
which one was it?

All the windows had blinds and curtains.

She went to the middle one. Not that one. Not the one
on the left.

At the final window, the ladder was attached to the
wall behind a small table her grandmother had used to
camouflage it.

Allie unlocked the window and pushed upward on the
sash. It didn't budge. Fear throttled through her veins.
She pushed again, using every ounce of strength she pos-
sessed. It didn't give.

The odor of smoke grew thicker.

Her lungs seemed to seize in anticipation of filling with
the deadly carbon and airborne particles. She had to hurry.
Think, Al.

What had she heard her grandmother say about old
windows being stuck? Sometimes the paint made them
stick… She needed something to slide between the sash
and the frame that held it in place.

Heart pounding, she rushed to the table on her grandfather's side of the bed, dragged open the drawer and
picked through the items there. He'd always collected and
carried pocketknives. She grabbed the largest one in the
drawer and rushed back to the window. It took her a moment to figure out how to open it. Once she did, she stuck
the blade between the sash and its frame and started to
wiggle it and then to slide it up and down. She did one
side before moving on to the other. By the time she'd fin-

ished, the smoke was thick in the air. Her body resisted the impulse to breathe.

She had to get out of here.

Dropping the knife, she got a grip on the sash with both hands and tugged. She groaned with the effort of lifting it, desperation rushing through her body.

The sash gave way, sliding upward a few inches.

Allie cried out with relief. She placed her hands beneath the lower part of the sash this time and pulled upward again and, thank God, up it went.

Her knees went weak with relief.

It took a few seconds to get the screen out of the way. She allowed it to fall to the ground outside. It was pitch dark in the backyard. She wished she'd turned on some exterior lights when she arrived and started turning on lights in the house.

She released the ladder and pushed it over the ledge and out the window.

Now all she had to do was climb down. She stuck her upper body out the window and stared toward the ground. It was quite a ways to fall.

"You can do this."

She could. She really could.

She drew her upper body back inside, next one leg went out the window, then the other. The position she'd chosen left her sitting on the window ledge with her legs hanging out. With a deep breath, she rolled onto her stomach and eased her lower body out farther.

Now her legs dangled in the air. The window casing cut into her abdomen.

She focused on finding the ladder with her feet. First one foot hooked on to a rung and then the other. Her heart in her throat, she tested her weight. No snap and break, no sudden drop. Okay. She started down. One rung at a time. Right. Left. Repeat.

When her feet were on the ground, she wilted against the side of the house.

She was down without breaking anything.

The fire blazed in the first floor windows.

Fear snaked around her throat.

The house would soon be fully engulfed.

The photo albums. Her family's things! Her entire history. Allie slapped her hands over her mouth to hold back the scream that burgeoned there.

But she couldn't scream. Whoever had set the fire could still be out there watching to make sure she went up in flames with the house.

She needed to call 911.

She reached into her pocket for her phone.

Not there.

Had she left it on her desk? In the SUV? Had it fallen on the floor in her grandparents' room or on the ground outside?

A loud sound in the front part of the house or on the porch shattered the air. Had a room caved in?

She had to get out of here. Find help. Get back to Steve.

After a quick glance side to side, she rushed into the wooded area between her house and the one next door. She ran through the trees, stumbled over things she couldn't identify in the dark. She ran until she reached the clearing that was the yard of the next house. It was dark. The occupants were either in bed or away.

Gasping for air and moving slowly, she made her way to the street. Fear pulsed in her veins. If she could make it across to the yellow house, she would knock on the door. The Simpsons lived there. They were friends of her grandparents. Their car was in the driveway.

She checked both ways then started across.

Just as she reached the halfway mark, a car barreled around the curve on her left.

She froze for an instant then turned and rushed back to her side of the street in hopes of reaching the cover of the trees before she was spotted.

The car skidded to a stop.

Not a car she realized. An SUV. Oh God.

She was about to dive into the woods when, "Hey, get in before they find you!"

Rivero.

A dozen questions shot through her head, but there was no time to analyze the situation. She could stay and hope to find a way out of here, or she could go with him.

She turned back to the street. The vehicle was his vintage Land Rover.

He could take her to Steve. Okay. She ran toward the vehicle, the door opened and she climbed inside. "They set my house on fire."

"Buckle up." He stamped on the gas, and the vehicle rocketed forward.

When they passed her house it was fully involved.

"Damn," he muttered.

"Everything is gone," she murmured. Her entire history was gone. Her family's history.

"At least you're alive." Rivero glanced in her direction.

She nodded, her body starting to shake from the receding adrenaline.

"You came for your laptop. Did you get a look at whatever you found?"

She nodded again, watching in the side mirror as her house disappeared in the distance as they drove away.

"I wish you hadn't looked." His words were spoken so quietly she almost didn't hear him.

"Why?" Her voice sounded weak and somehow frail. Everything was gone…her heart hurt.

He glanced at her again, his expression grim in the dim light from the dash. "Because you can't unsee it."

Chapter Thirteen

Tuesday, June 10
Woodstock Police Department
Lake Avenue, 12:05 a.m.

"I assure you, Mr. Durham," Special Agent Potter insisted, "this was a mistake. I checked in with my point of contact regarding your and Ms. Foster's activities, and he took me completely out of context."

"Trespassing," Steve said, rolling down his sleeves as they walked out of the building. "Vandalism."

"Well, you and Ms. Foster were digging on private property," she argued.

Alfred Mannington held up a hand. "I believe we've cleared this up, Agent Potter. I see no reason to continue with this discussion. Mr. Durham has been through enough tonight."

Mannington was the agency's top attorney. Steve hated to drag him down here at this hour, but he'd needed help in a hurry. Help with serious connections. Mannington was close friends with the governor as well as several other state representatives. Woodstock's chief of police was only too happy to put in an appearance to handle the situation.

Potter acknowledged Mannington's suggestion with a nod. "Very well. Good night, gentlemen."

Steve waited until she had climbed into her vehicle and driven away before turning to Mannington. "Can you give me a ride to the Foster home? When they returned my personal items, I had a text from Allie—about an hour and twenty minutes ago—saying she was running to her house for her laptop." He scanned the parking lot. "But she's not back, and that worries me."

"Sure thing."

As they strode to Mannington's sedan, Steve considered that as tired as Allie had been she might have fallen asleep at her desk or on the sofa. But he wasn't banking on anything that simple. She should be back by now. At the very least, she should be answering her phone, and she was not. He'd called twice.

Worry and outright fear had his pulse shifting into overdrive. He had promised her everything would be okay. She was safe with him.

He'd let her down.

Steve gave his colleague the directions as they drove. He could use a decent cup of coffee. The stuff back at the police station had been in the pot far too long. He'd drunk two bottles of water trying to get rid of the bitter taste. But coffee would have to wait. He had to find Allie and make sure she was safe first.

The instant they turned onto Allie's block, he spotted the emergency vehicles, lights blazing in the darkness. Neighbors had come out onto the sidewalks.

Fear grabbed him by the throat. "Oh hell." He leaned forward in an attempt to see more clearly.

Mannington slowed for the officer standing in the middle of the street blocking traffic.

The uniform came around to the driver-side window. "I'm afraid you can't—"

"That's my house," Steve interrupted him with the necessary lie to cut to the chase. "I have to get over there."

The officer stepped back and waved them through.

"This does not look good," Mannington pointed out.

"Park here." Steve was already opening the door when the car eased to the curb. He jumped out and rushed across the street.

More uniforms tried to stop him. He gave the same story, which got him directed to the man in charge.

"Can you tell me if anyone was home this evening?" the fire marshal asked.

Steve was grateful the man didn't ask for identification. His driver's license showed his address in Chicago. "My girlfriend was here." He spotted his SUV then. It was parked to the side and didn't appear to have been damaged. He would have felt better if it hadn't been here. "She drove my SUV here around ten thirty or so."

Despite the fear funneling inside him just now, somehow calling Allie his girlfriend felt right. At the same time, he was terrified she was hurt…or worse.

"Where were you?"

Steve pushed aside the distracting thoughts. He had expected the question. "I was at the police department. We've been looking into an old case." He put a hand against his chest. "I work for the Colby Agency in Chicago. I'm helping my girlfriend with the case. Anyway, I was speaking with Special Agent Potter from the FBI and Chief of Police Williams this evening. She needed to get home and…" He gestured to his SUV. "I need to know that she's okay."

What he needed was to get closer…to scream her name. To find her!

The fire marshal nodded. "Would this investigation

trigger something like this?" He indicated the burned-out house with his notepad.

Steve fought for patience. If he expected to be allowed anywhere near the house, he had to play the damned game. "Unfortunately, that's a strong possibility." The house—it was a total loss as was everything inside. The reality crashed into him again that Allie could have been in there. "I have to go in there. I have to make sure she's not in there."

The urgency was a palpable force inside him. He started for the house, but the fire marshal grabbed him by the arm and pulled him back.

"I'm afraid no one can go in there right now, sir. I don't mean to be insensitive, but if she was in there, it's too late to help her now."

Mannington was suddenly next to him. "We should let them do their jobs, Steve."

Steve wanted to punch them both and make a mad run for the house.

Two firefighters suddenly appeared. Steve's determination withered a little as he braced for bad news. How the hell had he allowed this to happen? He should never have let her out of his sight. This was on him. Damn it. This was his mistake. He should have asked for more help from the agency.

"Sir," one of the firefighters said to the marshal, "there's an emergency ladder around back coming down from one of the upstairs windows. Looks like whoever was in there released the ladder and either got out or tried to."

Hope flared in Steve's chest. He should have known better than to give up on Allie. She was a survivor. She wouldn't go down so easily.

"Have you searched the yard? The property goes into the woods. She could be out there injured," Steve demanded, hope daring to expand once more.

"We have, sir," the same firefighter said. "We've done all we can until things cool down a little." He held up a clear plastic evidence bag. "We found this on the ground near the ladder."

Allie's cell phone was in the bag. She had come down that ladder in a hurry, which would explain how she'd lost her phone and hadn't taken the time to look for it.

She'd feared someone who wanted to hurt her was close.

Steve reached for the bag. "May I see it?"

The fire marshal shook his head. "Afraid not, sir. This is evidence. We have every reason to believe this was arson."

"Please," Steve urged, "can you just show me the final text messages and phone calls?"

Mannington stepped into the conversation then. "This is a matter of life and death, Marshal. Time is of the essence. We need whatever we can find to point us in the right direction. Allie Foster is—" he gestured to the house "—as you can see, in danger."

The marshal passed the bag to Steve. To the two firefighters, he said, "You two are my witnesses if there's any trouble about this decision."

Yes sirs echoed from the pair.

The last call, besides the missed ones from him, was before they were pulled over and he ended up being hauled away in a police cruiser. The final text was one she'd sent to Steve, but the one before it was to Rivero, telling him she suspected she'd found something, and she was going to her house to have a look at it.

Fury chased away the cold uncertainty in Steve's gut. He passed the phone back to the marshal. "Thank you. Is there anything else I can do here to help?"

"I need your name and contact info," the marshal said. "Then it would be best if you got out of our way like your friend suggested."

Steve pointed to his SUV. "Can I take my vehicle?" He had no idea where the fob would be. He glanced at the house. Probably fried inside.

"Afraid not, sir. Anything close to the house has to be considered evidence in cases like this one."

Steve nodded. "Thanks anyway."

He and Mannington walked back to his car. "I think I know where she is," Steve told him. "The last text she sent to anyone besides me was to someone we've been interviewing."

Mannington looked at him over the top of the sedan. "I can call for a car. Take me to a diner or someplace I can hang out, and you can use my car. Find her. Do whatever you have to."

"Thanks, man, I appreciate it."

Mannington pointed a finger at him. "Do not wreck my car."

Steve smiled. "I won't get a scratch on it."

He drove Mannington to Red's. It was closed, but a quick call to Red had him waiting at the door to open up and keep Steve's colleague company.

Steve headed for Rivero's place. If the man tried to pretend he had no idea where Allie might be, Steve intended to beat the daylights out of him.

Chapter Fourteen

Madison Residence
Hamilton Road
Woodstock, 12:30 a.m.

Allie had a bad feeling something was going on with Rivero.

First, she had been stunned that he'd left his house to come to hers. Her impression was that he never left the house. Granted, maybe he was like her in that he preferred to stay home but wasn't a true recluse or agoraphobic.

The fact that he'd driven fast but competently and continued to speak fairly reasonably had assuaged her concerns. Still, she'd wanted to text or call Steve, but she'd lost her phone, and Rivero insisted he'd forgotten his in his haste to get to her house. The driving around in all sorts of directions for half an hour or so had seemed reasonable to ensure they weren't followed.

All that aside, it was when their frantic journey ended on the road to Thomas Madison's house that alarm bells were triggered.

"Why are we here?"

He pulled deep into the driveway, past the house and right up to the detached garage as if he'd been here before. She imagined he had. He'd been following this story for thirty years. Why wouldn't he have tracked down the Madisons and tried speaking with one or both.

"This is where it all came apart." He shut off the engine and turned to her.

The interior lights of his vehicle dimmed until they went completely dark. An exterior light on the detached garage provided some illumination—enough for her to see his face. He appeared calm now.

"I don't know what you mean." She worked on achieving her own state of calm. He didn't appear to have any sort of weapon. He hadn't threatened her. No reason to be concerned. She hoped.

He reached for his door handle. "Come on. We'll go inside, and I'll explain."

She climbed out and followed him toward the back of the house. "Do you think they had anyone watching my house who might have seen you pick me up? Should we be worried about our safety?"

At the back door, he hesitated. Swatted at the bugs swarming around the light next to it. "We're safe. I'm guessing whoever they hired to set your house on fire split as soon as the flames were going well enough to be confident the job was done."

"The job," she repeated, then swallowed with effort. "You mean eliminating me?"

He made a sound that wasn't quite a laugh, more a grunt. "What else? These guys are ruthless. I thought you got that part already."

"I suppose it's my eternal assumption that people are good that makes me seem naïve."

He shot her a look before opening the door. "Time to

leave the gullibility behind. There's no room for ignorant bliss in this situation."

She supposed he was right about that. There was no more deniability. Ledwell did bad things, and people, including her parents, had been murdered to protect their secrets.

Allie had lost everything.

Ledwell had taken it all from her.

They entered the house through a mudroom. Rivero flipped on lights as if he came here all the time. In the kitchen, he did the same, turning on the overhead light, which was one switch in a panel of six.

How had he known exactly which one to flip?

Tension worked its way through her, but she asked no questions. No need to give him a heads-up that she was suspicious again. If she was lucky, since the power was still on, maybe there was a landline in the house. She'd gotten rid of the landline at her house long ago, but some people preferred to keep them even with cell phones.

He turned to her. She jumped, just a little. She prayed he didn't notice.

The smile that appeared when she jumped was the oddest expression.

Oh yes, he had noticed.

"Let me show you around. There's something I think you should see."

She nodded. Summoned a smile. "Sure." Damn. That was not what he would expect her to say. She was in the home of Thomas Madison—her father's former friend and colleague. "I hope you found something that will help me prove Ledwell murdered my parents."

He glanced back at her as he strode toward the staircase. "Oh, I think you'll find this most interesting, and it will confirm everything you already think you know."

She followed him to the stairs. Rather than go up the staircase, which went both ways, he headed down.

The way the house was designed, there was a lower level that opened to the outside on the far end of the house. People often built houses with exterior access to a basement level when on a hillside. She and Steve had seen this when they were here before, but the window and door coverings had prevented them from seeing inside.

The lower level was pretty much what Allie had expected. A large den with a kitchenette and dining area. Wood floor, area rug, white walls. Well-used sectional and a television. An open door led to a bedroom. Allie could see one corner of the bed beyond the doorway. Another door on the opposite wall was different. More like a vault door with a keypad.

"You see," he said, sounding proud of himself, "this is what's going to blow you away."

Anticipation and a twinge of fear pricked her. She glanced around. No sign of a phone. Damn it. If she just ran, she might be able to outmaneuver him but maybe not. At least, right now, he had no idea she was suspicious. "What exactly are you about to show me?"

"You think that flash drive you found is interesting. Wait until you see this."

Did Thomas Madison have files locked away down here?

Wait. "You know what's on the flash drive?" She felt like biting her tongue after having asked the question, but this was growing more bizarre by the moment. Under the circumstances, it was a fair question.

He turned his hands up and gave a look that said *duh*. "I knew what they were doing. I just couldn't prove it."

She nodded slowly, her head trying to wrap around what he was actually saying. "You're here, in this house, and it seems like you've been here before. Had you and Thomas Madison become friends?"

He made a face. "I wouldn't say we were friends." He shrugged, glanced at the door. "I have a friend who works at the hospital who let me know he was not doing so well. He'd been in the hospital two other times over the past several months. His deteriorating condition was what brought me back to Woodstock."

Allie's heart rate started to climb. She wished she had found some way to get in touch with Steve. This was bad. She no longer had any doubts. This was really bad. Rivero was not trying to help them, and it didn't matter if he believed she was suspicious. This was not going to end well.

"The last time he was in the hospital, before his demise—" he shrugged "—about six weeks ago, I paid him a visit after he got home. The home health nurse was out smoking a cigarette, and I sneaked in. She never even knew I was here. I just hid and waited until she left. I'd parked my Rover at a house down the road. It's for sale, you know."

"I saw the sign," Allie said, going along. Her best chance of surviving this was to keep him believing she wasn't on to him until she could figure out a way to escape.

"I made my way through the woods and just waited for the right opportunity." He shrugged again. "What else do I have but time?"

He walked to the French doors and opened the blinds there. That was when she spotted his cell phone in the hip pocket of his jeans. Either that or he was carrying some other thin rectangular object the right size.

If she'd had any doubts, she now knew the bastard had lied to her. She wasn't surprised, just disappointed in herself for trusting him in the first place.

"We had quite the time catching up." He laughed, the sound just shy of evil. "His physical condition didn't allow him to force me out of his house or stop me from doing whatever I wanted. Tying him to the bed was easy enough. Of course, I had to do so carefully otherwise the nurse would have noticed any bruising."

"Smart," she said when he didn't immediately continue.

"He told me that it wasn't Ledwell who put out the hit on your father."

Allie drew back as if he'd slugged her. "But it's the only thing that makes sense. You said Ledwell was responsible for their deaths and numerous others."

"They are responsible. Just not directly. The CIA has always been at the top of everything they do."

"So it's the CIA." She held up her hands to put an end to this. She'd had enough. Whatever was about to happen, she just couldn't do this anymore. "Okay, Mr. Rivero. I really need to call my friend Steve. He'll be worried, and I'm really tired."

He pursed his lips and did some head shaking of his own. "Unfortunately, it's too late to turn back now."

"What does that mean, Mr. Rivero?" Fear started to ramp up inside her, but she refused to back down now. She had known it would go this way if she gave him any trouble. It was now or later. It wasn't like she could walk this back. "Are you threatening me? I thought we were on the same side."

He moved toward the door that looked like one on a

vault or large safe. "I've always been on my own side. There were times, I suppose, it seemed we were on the same one, but your definition and mine are clearly different."

"I'm done here." She could go across the street to that neighbor's house, the one who showed up when she and Steve were here before.

Rather than wait for his reaction, she walked away. She had reached the stairs when he stopped her with, "But then you won't see the proof you need to reveal who killed your parents. I can give you that."

Did she walk away and risk never knowing? She had the flash drive...but was it enough?

"Fine." She turned around. "But don't expect me to go into wherever that leads." She nodded to the door in front of him.

He laughed. "Don't worry. You don't have to go in."

No matter what he said, she opted to stay near the staircase. If she got uneasy again, she was out of here unless he physically stopped her. Frankly, at this point, she couldn't be sure what he intended. One moment she was convinced he planned to harm her, and the next she wasn't so sure.

He pulled the keypad free of the door, swinging it to one side. Then he reached into his pocket and retrieved something. A key, she realized, as he inserted it then gave it a twist, reached for the handle and opened it. The big, no question about it now, vault door opened.

"He wouldn't give me the code," he explained. "But I knew there would be a key somewhere. It took some time, but I found it."

"And what is it you believe I need to see?" She folded her arms over her middle in an effort to conceal the shaking that had started. She would not be afraid, she repeated silently.

"The most explosive secrets that Ledwell has are right here. A maze of files, including videos, and the perfect example of what they were and are still doing in the sub-levels of that high security lab."

"If you had access to this," she said, her anger rising again, "why the hell didn't you tell me. I wouldn't have been running around all over the place trying to find evidence." Another realization had her drawing back. Wait just one damned minute. "Why would you need the evidence my father had if you had access to this?"

"But you would've missed all the fun. And there is the small matter of tying up loose ends." He gestured to the room. "Have a look."

Ensuring that she stayed beyond arm's reach from him, she moved closer until she could see inside the room.

Bookshelves covered two walls, each lined with binders. Rows of filing cabinets stood against the other two walls. In the center of the room was a round table with four chairs.

A man suddenly appeared in the doorway, stepping from one side of the door as if he'd been hiding or cowering there.

"May I come out now?"

Allie stumbled back. The man inclined his head and stared at her. "Who is this?"

He was medium height and build. He had black hair and vibrant...*green* eyes.

The photos she had seen of Tommy Madison filled her head.

"Tommy?" The name slipped from her lips before she could catch it.

He frowned, stared at her. "Do I know you?"

"You don't know her," Rivero spoke up. "She's your target for today."

Allie's attention swung to him. "What did you say?"

Rivero smiled. "Don't mind me, I was just leaving. It was nice to have known you, Allie Foster. Thank you for finding that evidence and bringing it right to me. One less bit of housekeeping."

"What the hell are you doing?" she demanded.

Rivero paused in his obvious exit. He turned back to her. "I'm doing what I've waited twenty-eight years to do, leaving with all the loose ends accounted for so that I may live the rest of my life in peace."

Allie shook her head. "I don't understand."

He exhaled a put-upon breath. "If you must know, here you go. I was Ledwell's watchdog, so to speak. My career was on a downward spiral." He shrugged. "It happens. One day you're at the top, and the next someone younger and more handsome takes your spot. At any rate, I was in a bit of a pinch money wise, and I approached Ledwell with a proposition. I would keep the trouble from their door for the right price. They knew I was like a magnet to people who wanted to tell their stories."

Allie's chest constricted. "You lured in would-be whistle-blowers with your reputation for exposing the dirty laundry of big tech and politicians."

He smiled. "Smart girl. It was the easiest money I'd ever made. Every single one swallowed the bait. Except your father screwed me. He was supposed to have the evidence with him, not your mother. I never liked being responsible for the deaths of innocents."

She rushed toward him. He reared back in mock fear, laughing in her face.

"You killed them."

"Your father killed himself by betraying his employer. Killed his wife too. And he left me hanging. I had to disappear to prevent the same fate."

Fury twisted her lips. "Why did you bother coming back after all these years? Why didn't you just stay gone?"

"Well, you know what Dorothy said: There's no place like home. But I knew I could never come back…unless I found a way to make it right. What better way than to put it all on a dead man's shoulders? I only had to wait for him to die—well, I may have hastened it along. He was dying anyway. When the dust settles, I'll be able to get any price I want for my book, and no one, no one, will be able to touch me."

"I don't believe you." She had to keep him talking until she figured out some sort of new plan. "How could you have learned what was happening and then pulled all this off?

"I still have a few of my old contacts. I learned of a certain someone's failing health, and a plan came to me. I could kill two birds with one stone, as they say. With your grandparents long gone and you so lonely, all cooped up in that old house, I estimated you were ripe for the picking." He grinned. "I love it when I'm right." He glanced over her shoulder. "Well, it's past time I left. You two enjoy yourselves."

He turned and walked out the French doors.

Allie started after him. She wanted to tear into him. He slammed the door in her face and locked it. She reached to unlock it, but it was the type of lock that required a key. And he had that key.

"Damn it!"

She ran for the staircase.

"Where are you going?"

She dared to pause and look back. "I'm sorry, Tommy, but I have to leave." No matter that she would love to know how he was here…she had to get word to Steve. Rivero could not slip away again.

"Apologies," this man—Tommy—said, "but you cannot leave. I can't allow it. You are the target."

Allie started to ask what that meant, but she actually knew. No need to try buying time. So she rushed up the stairs instead.

The sound of his footfalls behind her echoed in her ears.

Rivero Residence
Lake Shore Drive, Wonder Lake, 2:00 a.m.

ALLIE WASN'T HERE.

Steve felt way beyond desperate. He had to find her.

Mannington had made another call to the chief of police, and every available uniform on the city's payroll was helping with the search. An APB had been issued for Rivero and his SUV.

Steve had even called Agent Potter for help. She and Fraser had shown up ASAP. He supposed he should appreciate the effort, but to his way of thinking, Allie wouldn't be missing if not for Potter's little game.

With the house fire and Allie missing, the chief had declared exigent circumstances and Rivero's home had been searched.

The bastard had all sorts of evidence related to Ledwell. He'd had it for years it seemed. Insurance? Blackmail? Whatever his game, it was not about getting evidence for his long overdue story or the book he claimed to have written. This was about something else entirely.

Two detectives had been sent to the home of Edgar Ledwell, the man who'd started the company. Several officers were posted outside the lab. Another pair of detectives had gone to the home of Ledwell's son, second in command at the renowned company. So far, no sign of Rivero, his vehicle or Allie.

"I think it's safe to say," Fraser spoke up, "that Rivero is on Ledwell's payroll."

Steve resisted the first response that came to mind. *You think?* Instead, he grunted an agreement. Right now, he cared about just one thing: finding Allie safe.

He swiped his forearm across his face to clear away the sweat. Fatigue tugged at him. He smelled of smoke and sweat from Allie's home. Fraser got a call and moved away. Steve watched as he motioned for Potter. The police were still searching the property.

Rivero had no other properties—at least none listed in his name.

Where the hell would he take her? And why? She had nothing in the way of concrete evidence unless what she'd found in that time capsule was significant.

Maybe that was the problem. Rivero might not want her to have it, particularly if he was working for Ledwell.

Steve swore again. He had to find that lowlife bastard.

In his pocket, his cell vibrated. He hoped to hell this was something, anything to help. The number wasn't one he recognized. No matter, he hit accept. Allie could be using someone else's phone. "Durham," he said in greeting.

"Mr. Durham, this is Gayle Fischer."

Madison's neighbor on Hamilton Road. The nosy one.

Why would she be calling at this hour? Hope rushed into his throat. "How can I help you, Mrs. Fischer?"

"Well, I don't know if this is anything, but just before 1:00 a.m. a vehicle went into Thomas's driveway. I might not have noticed it, but I was outside on the porch because I couldn't sleep. Insomnia is my companion all too often lately."

"Can you describe the vehicle?" Steve wasn't waiting, he walked to the car, scanning those around him to ensure no one noticed. He climbed behind the steering wheel and started the engine. He cringed at the sound, but no one paid the slightest attention.

"It was some sort of SUV. One of those foreign jobs. White, I think. I woke up my husband, and he said it had been there before, but sometimes he gets things wrong, so I watched."

Steve resisted gunning the engine. Instead, he rolled slowly and quietly away from the other vehicles gathered around Rivero's house. "Can you tell me if the vehicle is still there?"

"It left just a few minutes ago, and that's why I'm calling you."

He drove, moving faster as he put distance between him and the cluster of official vehicles. "Were you able to see who was in the vehicle?" If she'd seen Allie, that would explain her calling him instead of the police. Hope dared to swell in his chest.

"No. Unfortunately not. But after the SUV left, I walked over there to see if anything had been disturbed. Lights were on, so I approached with caution. I saw the woman who was with you the other day. She and a man were in the kitchen. It looked to me like they were just talking, but when she moved toward the door, he blocked her path. I don't know what's going on, but I think she might be in trouble."

"I'm on my way," Steve assured her.

"I'll stay where I can see them through the windows, but I don't think I should go inside," she said. "I don't want to have to shoot anybody, and I never could tolerate a man pushing a woman around."

As much as he wanted Allie protected, he said, "You shouldn't go inside, Mrs. Fischer. Stay back from sight. I'll be there in a few minutes. Call me back if anything changes."

"I will."

The call ended, and Steve pressed the accelerator even harder.

The faster he could get there, the sooner Allie would be safe. A part of him wanted to inform Potter and Fraser and the police, but he didn't have a handle on the situation. The last thing he wanted was for a show of force to put this guy into desperation mode. Better to go in quietly and assess what needed to happen.

Steve didn't stop for red lights. He just kept going.

He had to get there.

Now.

Chapter Fifteen

Madison Residence
Hamilton Road
Woodstock, 2:27 a.m.

"Why am I a target?" Allie struggled to maintain her composure. Strangely, it seemed staying calm made a difference.

"The answer is one I can't provide," Tommy said.

He sounded human. Maybe he was. She had no idea who that scumbag Rivero had been keeping locked downstairs. By his own admission, he came into this house after Thomas Madison's health became so bad he couldn't care for himself or defend himself. He'd been here often enough to know all the secrets of the home and its owner.

"What did that man who was here before, Rivero, do to your father?"

His brow lined in thought. "My father's time here was finished. I was supposed to go before him, but he grew too ill to perform the necessary dismantling. Mr. Rivero explained that he would be supervising my continued existence."

Allie tried to remember if Rivero had hit her on the head or drugged her somehow. This couldn't be happening.

She kept recalling the man who'd done the Madison

child's cremation saying that his eyes were missing, and now…

Allie looked directly into this man's eyes—the ones that looked exactly like that little boy's. But that was impossible. This person was…too human to be a robot?

"Is Rivero the one who made me a target?"

"Yes. He has that authority now."

Allie stared at the back door he had effectively blocked by standing in front of it.

"I need to go home, Tommy. Can you please just let me go home? Someone burned down my house, and I need to see if I can salvage anything."

She told herself she could talk her way out of this. This man—person, whatever he was—was about her same age, and if he had lived with the Madisons all this time, he surely understood how relationships worked. Could he experience emotions? Determine right from wrong?

Good grief, she should have done more research on the subject. She really had no idea how far the technology had advanced, much less how it worked.

"You cannot go home, Allie. You are the target, so your existence must be terminated. I'm sure you understand the decision is out of my hands."

Somehow she had to get past his sweet, boyish looks and the charm he emanated and understand that apparently he was a cold-blooded killer. She had to be prepared to defend herself.

With what? She surveyed the kitchen for a knife… anything.

Dear God…would a knife even work? Was it possible to stop him?

"I understand you're disturbed by this news. I suggest we make this as quick and painless as possible. There are a number of options. We can discuss them if you would like, or I can choose and surprise you."

Her heart quickened, started to pound. This was like a nightmare come to life. She wanted desperately to believe this was not actually happening...but it was. She was right here looking her would-be executioner in the eye.

He smiled suddenly. "I'm aware that you're thinking there has to be a way out of this. Anyone would think the same, but please be advised that I am faster than you. Much stronger than you and far more capable at the art of strategy."

She was screwed.

There was maybe a dozen feet between them. She stood just inside the wide cased opening that led from the living room into the kitchen area. He stood directly in front of the back door, blocking her escape. She'd made a run for it, dashing up the stairs and toward the back door, which generally didn't have as complicated a locking system as front doors.

He'd easily overtaken her, but instead of grabbing her, he'd rushed ahead of her and placed himself in her path.

Did that mean he liked to play with his targets?

"Have you had other targets before?"

He blinked, considered her question. "Yes, but only electronic ones. My father and I played games together. Sometimes I even allowed him to win."

Electronic games. Allie nodded. "So you haven't ever terminated a living being?"

"No. You are the first living being, as you say, I've encountered other than my parents and Mr. Rivero."

The pieces started to come together in her head. His parents had been devastated when their child died. The mother had said his father would bring him back. She made that promise because his father worked at a cutting-edge lab that was already building robots who looked human and behaved like humans.

What parent wouldn't do whatever necessary to have their child back?

But this was not a child…this was a grown man. Was this man/machine capable of growing, or had they built a new model as needed and transferred the necessary data?

Oh God, she felt ill.

Steadying herself, she tried another approach. "Tommy, I think there are rules about robots hurting humans. Did anyone talk to you about those rules? Mr. Rivero is a bad man, and what he has asked you to do is illegal and immoral."

"All targets are evil," he argued. "You are a target, and therefore you are evil. You must be eliminated."

"The targets you and your father eliminated were in games, not in real life."

"Mr. Rivero said the games have invaded real life now. We can no longer trust what we once thought was the difference between this life and those in games."

Well shoot. That scenario pretty much eliminated any hope of swaying him with reason. Okay. He talked about strategy. Well she had one. And only one, as far as she could see. "Your mother would not want you to do this. She was friends with my mother. You and I played together when we were children…at the other house—the one with the pool."

He gave her a knowing look. "Targets often make up stories to mislead."

Oh crap. "What about photo albums? Your mother kept photos. Where are they? I'll show you that I'm telling the truth."

Please, please let the woman have kept photos from before...before this Tommy.

"Turn around," he instructed, "walk into the living room and to your right. You will see a bookcase that contains our family albums."

If she turned her back, would he rush up behind her and strangle her or break her neck?

This is the only option, Al.

She took a breath and turned around, following his instructions exactly. Three rows of shelves were lined with photo albums. She searched for the ones from twenty-eight to thirty years ago.

"Here we go." She removed two then carried them to the coffee table. She sat in a chair that faced the sofa in hopes he would decide to sit there. No such luck. He crouched beside her.

It took only a moment to find the photos she needed of their parents together. She pointed to her parents. "That's my mother and father. Your mother, Jane, and my mother, Alice, were best friends. Your father, Thomas, worked at Ledwell with my father, Jerry."

He studied the photos. "Where are the ones of you and I?"

Allie reminded herself to breathe. "Well let's see if your mother kept any of those photos in here." She turned a page, then another. Fear crept up her spine when there were no photos of them. Still, she kept turning pages.

"This is the house—" she pointed to a photo of the house where the Madisons lived before "—where the pool is."

He nodded. "I know about the pool." He looked directly at her then. "I drowned there."

She nodded. "You did." She turned another page. There

was a whole page of photos with Tommy in them and two included her. Her relief was so profound she barely kept her wits about her. "See." Her voice squeaked a little. "I told you we played together when we were little."

He leaned closer and studied the photos. "You are correct." He studied her face. "Our families were friends. We were friends."

She summoned a smile. "We were."

He turned back to the photos in the album. "I was very sad when my mother died."

"Me too. My mother and father both died not long after these photos were taken."

"What happened to them?"

"They died in a car accident."

He considered her words. "Who took responsibility for you?"

"My grandparents, my mother's parents." Another thought occurred to her. "You have a grandmother. Did you know that?"

"I do not."

"Yes. You do." Allie flipped back several pages, the idea or maybe her desperation gaining momentum. "This is your grandmother." She pointed to a photo of Mrs. Talbert and Jane.

"She died when I was a child."

"No," Allie argued. "I saw her two days ago. She is alive, and she misses you very much."

"My father would not lie to me." Anger flashed in his eyes, echoed in his voice.

Maybe this particular part of her strategy hadn't been such a good one. "I think he may have been afraid she might accidently tell someone about you, so he had to keep you a secret from her and her a secret from you."

"Take me to see." He stood. "I will pause your termination until you do this for me."

Allie nodded. "We'll need a car."

"There is a car in the garage."

"All right." She closed the photo album. "But we have to wait until morning. She lives in a building where there are certain visiting hours. We can't go in the middle of the night like this."

Headlights swept across the front window.

Tommy moved to the window and stared out. "Someone is here."

Allie wished she knew what the best course of action was.

She should run while he was distracted. It could be Rivero coming back.

"A man is coming this way." Tommy turned around. "We should go downstairs."

Shouting outside drew Allie's attention beyond Tommy and to the window. Banging on the front door came next.

"Allie! Are you in there?"

Steve. She started for the door.

A strong hand clamped on her arm. "We cannot allow him inside."

Allie winced at his tightening grip. "This man is my friend. His name is Steve, and he isn't here to cause trouble. He wants to help."

"How can I be certain?"

"Why would I lie to you?"

"You are a target. Targets often lie."

"I told you Rivero is the one who lied," she reminded him.

"Allie! Are you in there?"

"Please," she urged. "Steve and I will see that you get to your grandmother, but you have to trust me. Please."

He released her.

Allie walked to the door and unlocked it.

Steve stared at her. "You okay?"

She nodded.

"Thank God."

She moistened her lips, struggled with whether she should tell him to run or...didn't matter, he wouldn't. "I think you should come in."

"Where's Rivero?" he asked as he stepped inside.

That was the moment Steve's gaze landed on the other person in the room.

Allie saw the recognition flare in his eyes. "Hello." He extended his hand. "I'm Steve. Durham. Steve Durham."

Tommy looked at his hand a moment then grasped it with his own. "Tommy. Madison. Tommy Madison."

Steve glanced at Allie. She explained, "Rivero introduced me to Tommy, and then he left."

Steve nodded. "I see."

"You're taking me to my grandmother," Tommy explained. "I have paused my termination of the target until I determine the accuracy of her statement."

"Rivero told him I'm today's target." Allie winced. "Like in a video game."

Steve looked to Tommy. "Then I guess we should get going."

"I explained," Allie said, to maintain some sense of continuity, "that it might be difficult to get in to see her before daylight."

"I can arrange an afterhours visit." Steve smiled at Tommy. "I'll make a call en route."

Tommy looked to her. "I am trusting you, Allie. We are friends."

She nodded. "We are."

They walked out of the house. Allie inhaled her first deep breath since Rivero turned on her and started spilling all the ugly details of his heinous betrayal of so many people.

On some level, she felt vindicated that she now knew her parents had been murdered by someone associated with Ledwell. And yet, her heart wanted to break with a new kind of grief.

Her parents had been murdered—stolen from her when she needed them most.

"You've ruined everything!"

Allie froze.

Rivero.

The gun he held was aimed at Allie. But he'd left. Had he been watching?

Steve stepped in front of her and warned, "Every law enforcement agent in the county is looking for you, Rivero."

Rivero shook his head. "Doesn't matter now. I had barely driven away when the call came. Ledwell has thrown me under the bus. Used me to do their bidding, and now they're refusing to protect me." He looked beyond Steve's shoulder, straight at Allie. "All because of you." His gaze slid back to Steve. "And the Colby Agency."

Despite the fear shrouding her, Allie understood one thing with complete certainty. Tommy was listening to this exchange, and he would analyze the words and come to conclusions. Whatever else happened, she needed to try and make sure he came to the right ones.

"If you hadn't set up the murder of my parents," she

railed at Rivero, "and all those other people, you wouldn't be in this situation. You are the one who told them who to go after time and time again."

"I did what they paid me to do," he growled, aiming at her head now. "Those people loved making all the money Ledwell paid them but didn't have the courage to recognize the significance of what the company was doing."

"Is that why you killed Thomas Madison and tried to pin it on me? To take out two problems with one swipe."

"That wasn't my call," he argued, "but it was the right one."

"But the person who ordered his termination only did so because you told them his health condition was a security risk," Allie argued, guessing basically.

"He had been a security risk for a long time, and the powers that be just didn't want to see it. I made sure they had to see what was right in front of them. He should have been eliminated when his wife died. He was basically worthless after that." He waved the gun at them. "Now, go back inside. We're not doing this out here."

Allie and Steve started walking in reverse, toward the house. Neither wanted to turn their back on this wacko.

Tommy followed their example.

Once they were inside, Rivero ordered, "On the floor, face down. All of you."

Steve shook his head. "You're wasting time. If you want any reasonable possibility of getting away before you're caught, you should have been gone long before now."

"On the floor," Rivero shouted.

"It is true?" Tommy stepped forward. "Did you see that my father was terminated?"

"On the floor, Tommy," Rivero said. "I'm in charge now. You must do as I say."

"Answer the question." Tommy took another step toward Rivero.

Rivero swung his weapon toward Tommy.

Steve made a move. Rushed him. The two struggled. The weapon discharged.

Allie grabbed the nearest object, a small sculpture on the table by the front window. She raised it to slam into Rivero.

The two men suddenly rolled to the right, and Steve had him pinned to the floor. The weapon had flown out of his hand. She tossed the statue aside, and it landed with a thump.

Before she could locate the weapon, Tommy had picked it up. He stared at the gun, then at Allie.

"You should let me hold the gun." Her heart thundered.

He stared at it a moment longer, then handed it to her. Her knees wobbled with relief.

Steve shouted over his shoulder, "I need something to restrain him."

"A moment please," Tommy said before rushing toward the kitchen.

"Grab my phone from my back pocket," Steve said, "and call 911."

"Gladly." Allie plucked his phone from his pocket and made the call.

Tommy returned with a dog leash. He thrust it at Steve. "We had a dog once."

"Thanks." Steve took the leash and secured the man.

Rather than rant and curse, Rivero said nothing. He was done, and he knew it.

Allie wasn't done by a long shot. She intended to see

that Ledwell was brought to justice for every life they had damaged or taken.

The determination she felt was bone deep...soul deep.

Foster Residence
Ridgeland Avenue
Woodstock, 1:30 p.m.

ONCE RIVERO WAS booked and both Steve and Allie had given their statements, they took Tommy to see his grandmother. Mrs. Talbert had been thrilled and humbled to meet him. She was a little confused about how he was here, but it would take time for the full ramifications of what had happened to sink in. The Colby Agency had called in a specialist from another AI research and development lab to determine how best to help Tommy. That expert would determine how to move forward with ensuring Tommy was properly cared for.

According to Fraser and Potter, Ledwell's son had spilled his guts. And, ironically, the CIA was claiming no knowledge or involvement whatsoever in the mess that was Ledwell Labs.

When there was nothing more they could do, Steve had driven to Allie's ruined home. They sat in the driveway staring at the damaged structure. She doubted there was much inside that could be salvaged. More than anything else, she regretted the loss of all those family photos. Thankfully, she had the few photos that had been in the time capsule. Her baby bracelet, shoe and spoon.

"You're going to be okay."

She turned to the man behind the steering wheel of the borrowed car. "You think so?"

He smiled wearily. "I know so."

They were both utterly exhausted. "Thank you. I'm glad you have so much faith in me."

"You're smart. You're determined." He leaned into the headrest. "And I plan on being around to see that you have everything you need to be okay."

A smile slid across her lips. "I like that plan."

He leaned toward her. "Good." Then he kissed her, one of those slow, sweet kisses.

When they drew apart just far enough to get their breath, Allie realized she desperately needed a shower and to brush her teeth. She must look a fright. And she was starving.

"I am starving," she confessed. The shower and all else could wait.

"We should drive over to Red's and order everything on the breakfast menu."

"At this hour, we might have to settle for lunch."

Steve smiled. "I think he'll make an exception for the two of us after what we've been through."

"Sounds great."

As he drove away from the place that would never again be her home, he said, "You need a place to stay until you decide what's next."

She sighed. God, she hadn't even thought of that. "I do."

"I know this great place in the city where there's an extra room."

She turned to him. "Are you serious?"

He glanced at her. "I am completely serious. That's what friends do."

"I guess it's a good thing we're friends."

He reached out and took her hand in his and rested it

on the console. "We are friends, and I want very much to explore the possibility of more."

She squeezed his hand. "I'm all in for further exploration."

Maybe she'd ignored her social life all this time because somewhere deep down she had known the right one was coming.

Allie couldn't wait to see what happened next.

* * * * *

Be sure to watch for another
Colby Agency: Next Generation story coming from
Debra Webb and Harlequin Intrigue next month!

Memory of Murder

Chapter One

Chicago
Monday, July 7
Colby Agency, 9:30 a.m.

Jamie Colby waited in her grandmother's office, the package sitting in her lap. Her fingers tapped out a tune on the box, which had gotten slightly battered in transit. The package and its contents had been in Jamie's possession for a mere three days, but already she was convinced of what needed to be done. Quickly, she reminded herself. This had to happen as soon as possible.

Somehow she would make the indomitable Victoria Colby-Camp see that her plan was a good one. A necessary one that had to be carried out, even if pro bono. The agency did pro bono work all the time. Did it really matter that the actual client was deceased?

Not in Jamie's opinion. The woman deserved to have her reputation restored. Some things transcended death.

The door opened, and Victoria breezed into the office and settled behind her desk. "Good morning." She smiled brightly as she always did whenever she saw Jamie for the first time each day.

Jamie adored her grandmother. Her entire life, Jamie had always known she wanted to be just like her.

No matter that she and Jamie had been working together now for nearly seven months, each day was like the first with her grandmother. Calling Victoria grandmother almost always confused anyone who met them for the first time. Primarily because Victoria looked far younger than her seventy-two years. The silver threaded through her black hair spoke of sophistication and wisdom rather than age. But it was her keen eyes that warned she was no little old lady.

Jamie smiled. "Good morning, Grandmother."

Victoria eyed the package in Jamie's lap. "I understand you have a special case under consideration."

So, Ian had spoken to her already. Jamie wasn't surprised. It wasn't as if she had told him not to tell Victoria. Perhaps he'd hoped to grease the wheels, so to speak. Ian Michaels was one of her grandmother's closest friends and colleagues. His recommendation would go a long way—assuming he leaned in Jamie's favor, and she suspected he would.

"Yes." Jamie stood. She placed the box on the edge of her grandmother's desk and removed the contents, piece by piece. First the handwritten journal. Then the photos, the newspaper clippings, a locket, Polaroid-type photos and the baby blanket—the sort of receiving blanket given at birth, usually by a hospital. A detailed letter from the accused killer had accompanied the box.

As Victoria shuffled through the photos, Jamie explained, "Mary Morton was charged with first-degree murder thirty years ago. She was sentenced to life in prison. At the time, she was pregnant, and the baby—a girl—was later born and subsequently taken from her.

Since Mary had no other family or close friends able or willing to take the child, she was introduced into the foster system."

Victoria moved on to the newspaper clippings. "Has the child—woman," she amended, "been contacted about her mother's death?"

Jamie nodded. "I spoke with the warden. He gives his best, by the way." Her grandmother knew everyone who was anyone in key positions in the state and no small number of VIPs across the country. "A notification was sent to her last known address. I checked out the address, and she does live there. There's every reason to believe she's aware of the situation."

Victoria reached for the journal. "Tell me why we should be interested in this convicted murderer's history."

Jamie resumed her seat. "At the time of the murder, Mary Morton was twenty-four years old. She had just completed her master's in teaching, and she was already employed at an elementary school in Crystal Lake. On a personal level, she was engaged to a law student set to graduate the upcoming year. His name was Neil Reed. Both Mary and Neil grew up in Crystal Lake. Her parents were deceased, but his still lived in the area."

"Reed was the victim in the murder case." Victoria placed the journal with the other items.

Obviously her grandmother had already looked into the details. Possibly a good sign.

"Yes. Mary insisted throughout the trial that she was innocent, but the preponderance of evidence was overwhelming. Her prints were on the murder weapon. She had blood on her clothes. Her court-appointed attorney—a man overwhelmed with cases—didn't stand a chance against the newly elected hotshot district attorney deter-

mined to make a name for himself. My impression is that
the case was decided even before a jury was selected."

Victoria picked up a newspaper clipping, considered it
a moment. "Why are we talking about this case, Jamie?
The poor woman, guilty or innocent, is dead. I really don't
see how we can help her."

"We can," Jamie countered. "Mary's greatest regret
was that she couldn't clear her name to prove to her only
child that she was not the daughter of a murderer. According to her letter, Mary didn't care if she was ever released.
She only wanted to clear her name for her daughter's sake.
Her attorney promised to appeal her conviction, but his
meager efforts proved futile. Still, Mary never gave up.
No matter how earnest her efforts, it was as if whatever
legal maneuvers she attempted were doomed from the
outset. Every single time, she was met with defeat. No
reporter ever showed interest in her story. Fate simply
turned a blind eye to her. I feel strongly that the justice
system let her down."

Victoria studied Jamie. "Or she was simply guilty, and
no one wanted to help change a righteous verdict."

"That's possible, yes. However, everyone—even the
guilty—has the right to petition for an appeal. But guilt
is not the sense I'm getting from what we have here."
She gestured to the contents of the box spread over her
grandmother's desk. "Just before she died, Mary had lost
all hope. She saw an article about you, Grandmother, and
the story gave her hope that there were still good people in
the world who might be able to help her. She put together
this package and asked that it be mailed to our office. An
indifferent guard never bothered to see that it was done.
But after her death, there was some question about why
all her personal items were missing, and another guard

discovered the box in an office. She checked the contents and then hand delivered it here."

Victoria continued to study her, waiting, apparently, for her to go on.

"After a thorough examination of all you see and a review of the available public information on the case, I feel compelled to open a case and assign an investigator."

"Who do you have in mind?" Victoria leaned forward and placed the items back in the box.

"Jack Brenner. He has extensive experience with cold cases. I believe if there is something to be found, he can find it."

Victoria sat back once more and resumed her analysis of Jamie. "Jack is an excellent choice."

Anticipation flared. "Is that a yes?"

"On one condition," Victoria countered.

Hesitation slowed Jamie's mental victory celebration. "What condition?"

"The daughter will be notified and asked to participate in the investigation. We're not going to do this without giving her an opportunity for input. In fact, I would prefer she be actively involved."

Jamie nodded. "Fair enough."

"Brief Jackson," Victoria went on. "When he's ready, have him reach out to the daughter and make an appointment to discuss the possibility."

Jamie stood. "Very well." She placed the items back into the box and picked it up. "Thank you. You won't regret your decision."

"I'm sure I won't."